PIECES OF THE PUZZLE

Greg Stone

PIECES OF THE PUZZLE

A Parable on Doubt and Reasonable Belief
in This Broken World

Greg Stone

God Bless, You,
Sarah!
Greg
Gal. 2:20

RIVER BIRCH PRESS

Mesa, Arizona

Pieces of the Puzzle by Greg Stone

ISBN 978-1-956365-54-2 (print)
ISBN 978-1-956365-55-9 (e-book)

For Worldwide Distribution
Printed in the U.S.A.

River Birch Press
P.O. Box 7341, Mesa, AZ 85216

To my wife, Jodi, who is a supreme piece of my puzzle
of why I believe. Her faith in Christ shows brightly
to everyone she meets, and her consistent
dedication amid many dark valleys
is an example and inspiration.
I love you!

Acknowledgment

A special thanks to Dr. Mark Rapinchuk, professor of Biblical and Theological Studies at College of the Ozarks in Point Lookout, Missouri, with an emphasis on Christian apologetics and philosophy, for his thoughtful insights and suggestions over this book.

Table of Contents

Prologue

I'm not sure I believe in God anymore.

This realization jolted my heart as I sat on my front porch overlooking the Ozark hills of my hometown. A fast cooling cup of coffee sat next to me on this early Saturday morning. I had awakened early, unable to go back to sleep. My wife remained in bed, worn out from her recent cancer treatments. I sighed, thinking of her suffering. *My sweet Mary.*

I was confused. Why would a God of love allow the suffering of innocent people like my wife? I could not find an easy answer. Perhaps my visit with my grandmother this morning would provide relief from my burden, a balm for my pain. My grandmother had always been that solace for me growing up. Her home, near ours, became a place of refuge and relief from the dark coldness of my house.

I gazed out over the hills, breathing in the fragrance of the morning and watching leaves slowly fluttering to the ground. Melancholy held me like a thick blanket. *If there is no God, this is meaninglessness. Life is a dead-end road, with suffering and struggling along the path. Maybe it would be better to accept this reality and try to enjoy the ride as best as possible.*

When I scanned the hills on the horizon, distant memories as a youth resurfaced. I would look on these same hills as a boy, with the nighttime stars dancing above, and remember feeling a sense of awe and wonder of the infinite. My faith back then, formed mainly by my grandmother, seemed simple and pure. Now, tainted by tragedy and the weariness of life, my faith felt hollow and broken.

My wife and I had not been able to have children yet, and

now I feared losing her. This fear gripped me constantly, from the moment I would wake up in the morning until I finally would fall asleep after a fitful battle. A strange mixture of doubt and anger toward God consumed me. One moment I decided He didn't exist, and the next moment I wanted to walk into the woods and scream at Him. Neither side had won out yet. I felt too tired to make the decision.

I sipped the last of my coffee. *If only I could make sense of this broken world. If only God would reveal Himself to me in a fresh, straightforward way. If only He would heal my wife and bring joy into our lives. Maybe then I would return to Him.*

Until then, I didn't have time for Him. I had enough on my plate.

"God, if you are real, show yourself," I whispered with a sigh.

I got up and returned to the house to get ready to see my grandmother. Dark circles were under my eyes, with darker clouds in my soul.

1

Grandma and a New Friend

I was preoccupied as I absently gazed at the road ahead. A combination of pines and multi-colored oaks reached out toward me as I drove by, waving a quick greeting. With my car windows down, the cool Missouri fall air felt crisp. The scent of burning leaves mingled with the wildflowers, offering their last whispers of sweetness.

I traveled this same route weekly on Saturday mornings to visit my dear grandmother. She resided in a nursing home on the edge of Berkley, a quaint town near Bull Shoals Lake in southern Missouri.

Mabel Brown, the mother to my father, Reuben Brown, spent countless hours pampering me as a boy. She and my grandfather, Leroy, lived a couple of miles away from our home near Stowville, six miles from Berkley. Mabel was the one who named me Wyatt. She had loved that name since she was a young girl, hearing the stories of Wyatt Earp, the famous western hero.

Mabel was also a deep believer in Jesus. I recall us sitting together at the small country Baptist church and singing old hymns. I can still smell the musty hymnals and the creaky oak pews. Her voice, though not exactly beautiful, rang joyous and loud as she sang. I often giggled instead of singing next to her, which usually resulted in a stern look from Grandma.

As I drove, thinking about those church services caused

me to frown. My relationship with God at one time had been close but now had drifted into the shadows. Various hardships in my life have caused seeds of doubt and discontentment to spring up and bear fruit in recent years. I sighed.

"God, where are you?" I asked under my breath.

I pulled into the nursing home parking lot. Another deep sigh escaped as I opened the car door. I always dreaded visiting my sweet Grandma Mabel in her weakened state. But at the same time, I reminded myself it brought her such joy to see me.

I opened the front door and stepped inside. Usually, I walked past other residents, focused on going straight to Grandma's room. However, for some reason, this time I stopped and looked around. Wheelchairs dotted the open room, with some people slumped over and others staring into space.

I looked in a corner of the room and noticed a grey-haired, bearded black man sitting with a cardboard table in front of him. It looked as if he were working on a puzzle.

I did not grow up knowing black men or women. Our county was decidedly white, and racist remarks were commonplace in homes and barbershops.

I quickly removed my gaze from him to the hallway ahead, where my grandmother usually lay in bed and walked slowly towards her quiet room and entered. She lay in peaceful sleep, her breathing gentle and her white hair lying on her shoulders. I sat beside her and stared at her.

I recalled when I picked strawberries with her behind their house when I was about seven years old. Grandma let me sell the berries for a dollar a quart at the farmer's market in downtown Berkley. I used that money to buy baseball cards.

Grandma Mabel's eyes fluttered open, and she smiled.

"Well, hello there, Wyatt!"

"Hi, Grandma. How are you?"

Grandma sighed. "I'm fine. Just passing the time. How's my grandson doing?"

"I'm fine." I lied. "Just been working a lot."

"You still working at Walmart? They made you the head manager yet?"

I shook my head. "No, not quite yet. I am assistant manager overseeing sporting goods."

"Well, that's good," Grandma said and grinned. "I'm sure proud of you!"

I leaned closer and gently placed my hand in Grandma's. "Have you been eating good?"

She frowned. "Oh, I try. I just don't seem to have my appetite lately."

"Make sure you eat well, Grandma. It will give you strength."

Grandma smiled. "You always look out for me, don't you, Wyatt? You have since you were a little boy!"

"Well . . . you're my grandma." I smiled back. "I love you!"

"I love you too, sweetie."

We talked for a while longer until I could tell she was slowly drifting back to sleep. As I quietly stepped out of the room, I could hear her beginning to snore. I remembered that snore on many happy nights sleeping over at her house.

I stepped out into the large room at the nursing home entrance and glanced again at the black man at the card table. He was staring at me, smiling. I decided to go over and briefly say hi. A strange curiosity was coming over me.

As I moved closer, I observed the man. His hair was white

with a short-cropped white beard and mustache. He sat in a wheelchair, but his hands and arms moved easily with his puzzle pieces. His black and leathery skin spoke of many years of living, perhaps difficult years.

"How are you doing?" I asked as I walked up to him.

"Well, now, I'd be doing a lot better if I could find this last corner piece."

"There it is right there." I pointed with my finger at the pile of pieces in front of him.

"Well, dang! It was right in front of my tired old eyes the whole time!" He picked up the piece and gently pressed it onto his emerging border pieces.

He then quickly reached out his hand toward mine.

"My name is Marcus Francis. What's yours, young man?"

"Wyatt Brown, sir."

"Please to meet you, Wyatt. Who did you come to see today?"

"My grandmother, Mable Brown."

Marcus smiled. "Oh, she's a fine lady. A fine lady indeed! How was your visit?"

"It was good. She was tired though, so we cut it short."

"Well, I'm sure she was glad to see you, Wyatt. It's always nice to get visitors!"

Marcus motioned to the chair across from where he sat.

"Sit for a while if you have the time. I don't get many visitors myself these days."

I was intrigued by this engaging man, so I obeyed and sat.

"Now, tell me, Wyatt, what do you do for a living?"

"I'm an assistant manager at Walmart in Branson."

"Well, look at you! A manager and all! Bet that keeps you busy!" Marcus' eyes sparkled as he spoke.

"Yes, sir. I put in full days for sure!"

"Are you married?"

"Yes, my wife, Julie, and I have been married for two years."

"Any kiddos?"

"No, not yet. We do want to have kids eventually though."

Marcus smiled. "Yes, kids are a wonderful gift from God."

I enjoyed this man. He was easy to talk to, and his eyes were kind. His mention of God, however, caused me to wince.

"May I ask why you are here, Marcus? You seem so healthy other than your wheelchair."

Marcus sighed. "Well, now. I am in better shape than most here, I admit. But I don't have much family anymore to look after me, and I don't want to be a bother to others since my stroke."

"You had a stroke?"

"Yes, sir. About five years ago, I think. Couldn't use my right side for a couple of years. Much better now, though I still have a hard time walking. Thus, the wheelchair."

I smiled. "Well, you sure seem to have your wits about you still."

Marcus laughed. "Well, now. The good Lord has allowed me to keep that for sure!"

"Do you have a wife and kids?"

Marcus' smile vanished. "I did have a beautiful wife of forty-eight years. My dear Cassie. She passed away about ten years ago. The Lord gave us two sons. They both live out of state with their own families."

"Do you ever hear from them?"

"Oh, they call me a couple of times a month. They are good boys but very busy living their lives. I got four grandkids I get to hear from too!" His smile returned.

I smiled and sat in silence. I admired this man for his

positive spirit. It didn't seem fair that he was here with his wife gone and his kids far away. My smile left me as old wounds of my own came to my mind.

Marcus seemed to notice.

"So, enough about me, young man. Tell me more about yourself. Are you happy?"

The directness of his question surprised me.

"Wow . . . Happy? I can't say that I'm truly happy, to be honest. Life has been pretty confusing for me lately."

Marcus put down a puzzle piece and leaned closer to me.

"What has been confusing, Wyatt?"

I sighed. "I grew up going to church and hearing about God and became a follower when I was a young teenager. Since then, I've encountered so much frustration and confusion from life." My words poured out in a bitter tone. Marcus noticed.

"I see. I see. And I understand, son. This fallen world can be awful hard. Awful hard. I'm not going to pry today and ask you all the details of your frustrations and confusion. But know if you need a friend to talk with, I'm always here. Right here, working on this puzzle!" He patted my hand as he spoke.

"Thank you, Marcus. I might take you up on that. To be honest, I just can't make sense of life right now. I don't even know if I believe in God anymore."

Marcus grabbed my hand gently.

"Do you want to know what I used to do before coming here?"

"Sure, I'd love to know."

"Well, sir, I was a professor at a university. A Bible professor! All those years teaching the Bible and spending time preparing for my lessons, I must say at times I struggled myself believing the words of the Good Book. Like you, life for me at times was hard beginning when I was a boy living a poor life down in Arkansas. I gotta tell you, I didn't like white people back then. Still have a hard time, to be honest. Some of the workers here avoid me because I'm black. But here I am talking with you now! Through it all, I learned something. You want to know what I learned, Wyatt?"

Marcus was looking right into my eyes. His eyes had grown moist with passion.

"What did you learn?" I asked, half afraid of his answer and yet mesmerized.

Marcus picked up his puzzle piece again. "Well, sir, I learned this."

He gently shook the piece.

"I learned that like this puzzle piece, and like all these other pieces, life has many pieces, or clues to truth, that all point to the greater picture of who God is, and the purpose of life. Just focusing on the pieces of the puzzle brings confusion and frustration. But putting the pieces together gives one clarity and understanding. If you will take a little time during your visits to your grandma to come see me, I'll share about the different pieces and why they help me believe in God and find hope in Him."

My heart pounded suddenly. Emotion tried to escape.

"Yes, I'd like that" was all I could say.

"Good. Good. And maybe you can help me finish this blasted puzzle here as well!"

I grasped my new friend's hand before leaving the building.

Walking to my car, I shook my head. *What an intriguing man this Marcus Francis is.*

Backing my car up and leaving the parking lot, heading

toward home, my thoughts ran back over our conversation. *Do I really want to open my heart up to Marcus? Do I like to think about God, life, and my broken pieces?* I shook my head. My life was like that puzzle, except it just seemed my pieces didn't fit together well. *Does my life have any deep meaning? If so, why aren't my pieces fitting together?*

I drove home in silence.

2

Why Pieces?

"Hurry up, Wyatt! We're going to be late!" my mother yelled from outside my room. It was another Sunday morning. I remember I was about ten, but I recall those same conversations from the ages of six to thirteen. My mom and dad, filled with stress, loaded me and my two brothers and sister in the car to go to church.

The ride to church lasted about twenty minutes. Usually Mom and Dad either rode silently or yelled at each other about the church, us, finances, or what we were doing after church. On this day, when we arrived in the church parking lot, I quickly exited the car, grateful for a few moments of quiet before we walked into the church building.

My parents' demeanor quickly changed as soon as we entered the doors.

"Hello, Suzie!" my mom exclaimed with a big smile on her face. "How are you?"

Dad smiled too but spoke little, ushering us kids quickly inside to find seats near the back as Mom continued visiting.

The same charade happened outside of our church. With neighbors, our parents seemed helpful and friendly. My dad always offered to help a neighbor fix a fence or move a new washer and dryer in a house. Mom liked to visit and help with our next-door neighbor, an elderly retired nurse named Ellen. She had lost her husband to a heart attack the year before and relied on Mom for her company and help around the house.

But when our doors were shut, and it was just us and Mom and Dad, their personalities took a grimmer tone. I didn't hear much laughter from them, and their conversations with each other always seemed either very formal and brief or biting and sarcastic. Mom showed kindness to us kids when she was in good spirits, but when she woke up angry, we avoided her. Dad usually kept to himself.

These memories surfaced as I sat on my porch, sipping my morning coffee. I reflected on my conversation with Marcus the day before and his comment about life being like his puzzle, with the different pieces being part of the bigger image. Considering my own picture, my pieces seemed jagged and dark, with an unclear picture. *If God exists, why would He allow my life to be so bleak and frustrating?*

I shook my head. I felt like my puzzle pieces were not all on the table but scattered and lost in a hundred directions. Over time, I grew disinterested in putting my pieces together. They never seemed to fit as they once did. *Why?*

So many pieces.

I sat beside my new friend, Marcus. Thoughts of my childhood had run through my mind on my way to the nursing home. My visit with Grandma felt short but sweet. Now I sat with Marcus, watching him again with his puzzle and wondering why my life was such a confusing mess.

"It's good to see you again, Wyatt," Marcus said, smiling. "How are you today?"

I marveled at Marcus' smile. For an older man, his teeth looked in excellent health, white and straight. His eyes sparkled through his glasses as he spoke.

"I'm doing okay, Marcus. A little down to be honest."

"And why is that?" Marcus leaned closer to me.

I sighed. "I'm just struggling with why this life I've been living seems so disjointed. I mean, it just doesn't make sense." I looked down, watching my hands in my lap clasped together, thumbs twirling in a circle.

"I see. I see." Marcus looked straight at me with a thoughtful stare while stroking his beard. "What parts don't make sense, Wyatt?"

I sighed again. "Too many to share in one conversation."

"Let's start with what is on your mind right now."

"Okay. On the way over here, I thought about my parents. They professed to be strong Christians in public, but at home were anything but with us kids and each other. I saw such hypocrisy growing up."

Marcus shook his head slowly. "And that confused you as a boy, I'm sure."

"Yes, it did. It made me wonder if God was really real, why I didn't see more change in my parents."

Marcus stared at me for a moment. "I'm sorry about that, Wyatt. I've always said the biggest obstacle for folks to see Christ are Christians. I've encountered lots of white Christians over the years who didn't show black folks the love of Christ, that's for sure."

I thought about what Marcus had just said. Indeed, my struggles with my belief in God stemmed from my parents and other followers of Christ over the years, who let me down in various ways. Those broken pieces further clouded my picture of a loving God.

"Wyatt," Marcus said, interrupting my thoughts.

"Yes, I'm sorry, Marcus."

"If your focus of belief rests on the perfection of broken people, you will always be disappointed. We have a broken world because we are broken people. When we learn to accept this, our expectations of perfection will melt away."

I knew Marcus was right on this, but it still didn't remove the pain.

Marcus picked up a piece of his puzzle. "Wyatt, we're going to talk about different pieces of life's puzzle and why I believe these pieces, when put together, form a strong picture on the reality of God and His influence on our lives. But before we get to that, it's important to understand that this world itself is in pieces."

"What do you mean?"

"Just what we've been talking about. People letting us down. Hypocrisy, hatred, and racism. Just watch the news each night. Murders, violence, lies, and cheating. All of these examples are a result of our world being broken to pieces by sin."

"I heard the word 'sin' a lot in church," I said. "What does it really mean, Marcus?"

"Good question, Wyatt. Sin is basically man saying to God, 'I'm going to go my own way and not follow you.' From this simple act of rebellion flows all the brokenness you see and experience in this world."

"So, you believe sin is us walking away from God instead of following Him?"

"Precisely, Wyatt. Sin started when Adam and Eve ate from the tree God forbid them to eat from. They chose to trust in the serpent's lies instead of believing God's wisdom and discretion. All of us are born into this first rebellion."

On my drive home, my thoughts returned to my childhood.

I was the middle child of three boys. Tom was the oldest, four years older than me. Bryce was two years older than me, and Sharon, the youngest, was three years younger. We fought as most siblings do and teased each other daily. But we enjoyed being together and stuck by each other when Mom or Dad raged. Mostly Mom. Again, Dad mainly stayed to himself, removed from the rest of us.

Tom, as the oldest one, bossed us around a lot. He seemed closest to Mom. She relied on him to keep us in line, which he seemed to relish.

Bryce and I played together and were very competitive. We played one-on-one basketball, raced on our bikes, and wrestled often. Being older, he always won, but that didn't stop me from trying.

Sharon smiled a lot, speaking quietly and gently. All three boys were very protective of her, though we still teased her for being a girl.

Grandma Mabel loved having us over to her house. She would cook the most amazing meals and would always have dessert. I remember the smell of her freshly baked peach cobblers. A hug from Grandma with her apron on enveloped us with warmth and scents of bread and love.

Sharon especially loved being with Grandma. Grandma taught her to cook, sew, and garden. They were kindred spirits.

I sure miss Sharon.

I pulled into my driveway and stepped out of the car. My mind whirled, thinking of my visit with Grandma and especially Marcus. This strange man with different-colored skin had come into my life when I needed an older, wiser friend. Not only did I have questions about God and His existence, but my heart also felt shattered with past hurts and present fears over my sweet wife, Mary.

She lay on the couch, sick from another chemo treatment. I sat next to her and placed her head on my lap. I stroked her hair and gently rubbed her aching head. The chemo treatment always gave her a headache with bouts of nausea. I stared at Mary's tender face, her eyes closed, with slight creases in her face from the pain. Her brownish blond hair, thinning from the treatments, lay over my knee. Part of my recent doubts about God rested on the suffering of this precious soul. *Why my Mary?* I shook my head and sighed.

"Are you all right?" Mary asked, her eyes flickering open.

"Yes, I'm fine." I lied.

"How was Grandma?"

"She was sleepy today but seemed in good spirits."

"Did you visit with that older man again?"

"Yes, I saw Marcus. We had a good visit. He's a pretty smart fella."

"What did you talk about?"

I sighed. "He's an old Bible professor and wants to talk with me about why he believes in God and Jesus."

Mary smiled. "Good. I'm glad you met him, Wyatt."

My Mary has a strong belief in God. Even with her cancer, her faith does not waver as mine does. I have often come home and seen her reading her Bible or listening to Christian music. Her faith is not loud or boisterous. It is quiet and gentle, yet strong and sure. I envy her.

"I have to admit, I was nervous talking with him at first, partly because he's black," I said, stroking her hair.

Mary gave me a questioning look. "Why?"

"I don't know. I just never have been around people of color before. I will say, Marcus put me at ease very quickly. My color didn't seem to matter at all to him."

Mary reached up and patted my arm. "Remember, Wyatt. God made all of us. We are all unique and precious to Him. It doesn't matter the color of your skin. I'm glad you and Marcus have become friends."

"Me too," I said. I meant it. Deep in my heart, I knew I needed help with the puzzle of my life. Maybe God, if He is real, brought Marcus into my life to help me.

3

The Design Piece

"Hello, Grandma!" I said with a smile as I walked into her room.

Grandma sat in a recliner chair, crocheting, with her feet up near her bed. She looked over at me and smiled. It brought back memories of sitting at her feet playing while she crocheted and hummed. Such peaceful memories.

"Hello there, dear Wyatt!" she said, dropping her needles in her lap.

I leaned over, kissed her on her forehead, and gave her a gentle hug.

"I heard you have met Mr. Marcus. What do you think of him?"

"He's a very nice man," I said, scooting a chair close to her. "Very interesting."

"Yes, he's very smart. He said he hopes you visit with him when you come see me."

"I plan to, Grandma. Going to help him with his puzzle!"

She laughed. "He's been working on that silly puzzle for quite some time. He could use the help!"

I visited with Grandma for over an hour, catching up on her visits with other family members and friends at the nursing home. She seemed to be feeling well and was in a cheerful mood.

I stepped out of her room and made my way to the big

room, expecting to see Marcus. The chair where he normally sat was empty. A nurse noticed me.

"Marcus is outside under the big maple tree," she said.

"Thank you." I quickly walked outside.

Marcus was sitting there looking up at the tree's branches. As I approached, he smiled broadly.

"Hello there, Wyatt! I'm so glad to see you!"

"Hello, Marcus. I'm surprised you're not working on your puzzle!"

Marcus chuckled. "I had to give it a rest. Besides, it's a beautiful day. Thought I'd enjoy God's creation for a while. I got a chair right here. Come join me, son!"

I sat beside Marcus and gazed up at the tree with him.

"This ol' tree must be 150 years old," Marcus said, letting a slow whistle out. "I bet he has lots of stories he could tell."

I stared at the tree. It brought me back to our home and the maple we used to climb as kids. That tree had stories it could recount as well, some I did not want shared.

I turned my gaze to Marcus. The dark skin on his face was lined deep with years, much like the tree. *What stories must there be with this kind, older man?*

Marcus looked at me and smiled. He pulled a piece of a puzzle from his shirt pocket.

"Are you ready to talk about the first piece of the puzzle of why I believe in God?"

I laughed. "Do you always carry puzzle pieces around with you?"

Marcus chuckled. "Well, now, only when I'm making a point!"

He turned the piece over in his hand, staring at it. "This here piece I call design."

He leaned toward me now. I could tell he was thinking deeply. He traced his finger around the edges of the puzzle piece.

"You see this piece here, Wyatt? It has a specific design and purpose. It has paint on one side of it and specific curves and grooves to fit with other pieces. Would you say this piece of puzzle was made by someone for a purpose, or did it just happen to be?"

"It's obvious someone made it, Marcus. Especially when you see it fit with other pieces."

"Exactly!" Marcus said, his eyes lighting up and his hands making fists, pumping with passion. "As I look at this puzzle piece, I see definite design and purpose. As I look at this here tree, I see definite design and purpose. And as I look at you, Wyatt Brown, I see specific design and purpose."

After putting the puzzle piece back in his shirt pocket, Marcus suddenly grabbed my hands with his. Turning them over palm up, he looked at me earnestly.

"Wyatt, did you know that no person who lives today or who has ever lived has had the exact same fingerprints you have on your hands? You are no carbon copy, my friend! You are no accident!"

I stared at my fingers and the faint prints. I have heard many times about how our fingerprints are unique only to us, just as the iris and retina patterns of our eyes, the rim of our ears, and our lip and tongue prints are unique.

Marcus released my hands. "I've always loved the study of astronomy and biology, Wyatt." He looked up at the sky. "Astronomy shows us the amazing complexity and design of our immense universe and the intricate design of how we can have life on this planet. And biology has shown the amazing complexity and design in our inner universe, from how our organ systems function together to the amazing world inside each of our cells."

We both sat in silence, again staring up at the tree. I took a deep breath, smelling the fragrance of nearby flowers and feeling the warm breeze against my skin. My head confirmed the truth of Marcus' words, but my heart kept its wall up. I sighed.

Marcus, still looking up, spoke again. "For myself, God's design is one of the main corner pieces of the puzzle of why I believe. It's the frame and clear evidence that beyond all the causes of life, from the farthest galaxies to the DNA in you and me, there is a great Causer behind it."

"But who or what caused God?" I was surprised at my question since I had heard the answer countless times in my upbringing at church.

"Ahh . . . good question, Wyatt! Yes, who caused or made God?"

Marcus smiled while still staring at his tree. "When you think about it, there really are two choices. One, someone or something caused God, but then something or someone would have caused that which caused God, and on and on this process goes on forever. Or, God is the uncaused Causer, outside of our space and time. God was, God is, and God always will be. He is beyond time and space. Those are our choices, Wyatt. Which makes more sense to you?"

I did not answer right away. Marcus' explanation made sense, but the idea of an entity always being present and not having a beginning was beyond my understanding. Logically, the idea of an ongoing process of cause and effect with no starting point seemed harder to comprehend.

"Both are hard to fathom," I finally answered. "But it seems having a Creator with no beginning seems easier to picture in my mind."

"Me too, Wyatt." Marcus smiled. "Me too."

"And remember," he suddenly continued, "science has shown with great certainty that our vast universe had a beginning point or a cause. The Big Bang Theory shows us that our universe is not eternal. It too had a start. The question is this: Who or what started the universe? I say, as it says in Genesis, the first book of the Bible, 'In the beginning, God.'"

Marcus smiled and nodded as he looked again up to the sky.

"As you study creation, Wyatt, it shows us a great deal about the type of being capable of creating such a universe. Understand also that the presence of functional information, like everything about our creation, always shows the product of intelligence."

This made sense to me. The evidence for the universe having a beginning point, that time and space started from a tiny speck, then exactly was sent forth at an incredible event, has been confirmed by many scientists, both atheists and theists. For the universe with time and space to have a start means logically that something or someone outside of our known universe started the process and that this Creator showed extraordinary intelligence in what was created.

Marcus looked at me. "And we haven't even talked yet about the amazing design inside of you and me!"

"What do you mean?"

Marcus gently poked my chest. "Inside of you and me, the Lord's great design is even more miraculous than His design of the universe. The way our organs and systems work together is simply amazing! And the wonder of our brain, my oh my!"

I nodded. I enjoyed biology in school and was fascinated with the complexity of the world inside each of us. Especially DNA.

As if reading my mind, Marcus continued. "Way back when Darwin wrote his theory of evolution, his understanding, along with others in his day, of our human cell was that inside each cell was a gooey, mysterious mass. Today, we know that an amazing, complex world exists in each cell, including the blueprint for life, DNA."

Again, I nodded. "Yes, DNA is pretty amazing."

Marcus whistled. "You're telling me! You take the blueprints for a house. Pretty detailed, showing where each door and window is to be placed, and their exact dimensions. Far, far more complex is the DNA in each of us. It gives detailed instructions on how each one of us is to be from a physical standpoint to the hairs on our head. And let me ask you, Wyatt, if someone were to hand you a blueprint for your house, would you ever suspect all those details got there by random chance? No! You would know beyond a reasonable doubt that the blueprint had to have a designer, or architect, who made the designs for your house. Why do people believe the DNA blueprint specifically for each of us could come by random chance? No, we had to come by a Master Architect or Designer. I say that Designer is God."

Marcus grew more excited as he spoke, his eyes shining with passion. His words rang true to me. They were logical, coherent, and clear. But hurt and old wounds clouded the clarity.

I sighed.

Marcus stared at me. "What are you thinking, Wyatt?"

I hesitated. "Your words are true, Marcus, I know. But it's hard to fully accept that there is a great Designer when we can't see Him . . . When His design is so . . . flawed."

Marcus patted my leg and nodded. "So true, Wyatt. As we look at the pieces, I believe other pieces are there that don't make the picture as clear but also need to be accounted for. For myself, one of those is tragedy and hurt. I believe that is the case for you too. All of us deal with tragedy and hurt. There's no escaping it. And if we focus only on those pieces of the puzzle, the picture will indeed become much less clear as to the meaning and purpose of life."

"Yes!" I agreed, suddenly angry. "You say there's a great Designer. And so there may be. But look at what He has designed. Even if He's real, why would He design such a crappy world?" My voice broke, and I was surprised by my emotion.

Marcus did not respond immediately. Instead, he patted my leg again and nodded.

After a long pause, he said, "Fair question. Fair question."

We sat in silence. I expected a defensive answer from Marcus. Instead, I got his presence. As I thought about it on my drive home, that moment with him was more important to me than his response. In this journey I was taking with my new friend, I realized it would sometimes be a painful journey, unpacking the root reasons for my doubts and unbelief. I sighed as I drove. *Am I ready for this?*

4

Broken Pieces

"Wyatt, have you heard about Carissa?" my friend Ronnie asked from the other end of the phone.

I was seventeen years old. I had just gotten off work, bagging groceries at the local Piggly Wiggly.

"No, what happened?" I said.

"She died in a car accident this morning."

My heart sank.

Carissa was a couple of years older than me but a lifelong friend from school. She always treated me kindly and liked to tease me. One moment she was in this world, on the cusp of adulthood, then she was gone.

I remember going to her funeral. I had never been to a funeral before. My parents always guarded us from tragedy. When my mother's sister died from cancer, they did not bring us to the funeral.

My knees shook as I walked up to see Carissa's lifeless body in her casket. Her chest had been crushed from the impact of her accident, but her face had not been touched. I gazed at her sweet face, now pale and silent. It scared me.

Suddenly, a thought popped into my head as I stared at my dead friend: *There you will be someday. Then what?*

My knees buckled as I walked away from the casket. Unable to speak because of my fright, I drove home. Alone that night in bed, I cried out to God, begging Him not to send me to hell when I died. I prayed to receive Christ into my life, acknowledging my need for a Savior for my sins.

I remember feeling a sense of relief and peace that I no longer needed to fear death and that I was, indeed, forgiven. I began going to church weekly on my own. I started reading my Bible nightly before bed, committed to following Jesus through this broken and scary world.

However, a new sadness enveloped me just a couple of months later. My dad, always the quiet one, suddenly wasn't home after I got back from my summer job. I asked Mom where he was.

"Your dad left this morning, Wyatt," she said matter-of-factly. "He's not coming back. We're getting a divorce."

And just like that, my dad was gone. No visits. No seeing him at my ballgames in the fall. He left our town and moved somewhere else. We did not know where. I never heard from him again. My mom retreated from us kids, depression covering her like a dark shroud, protecting her from further pain and withholding her from tender love. Her distance became a cold, mechanical relationship with us that caused us to look for ways not to be home.

I sighed. The tragedy of those two events happened over nine years ago but was still fresh in my mind. The feelings of betrayal from my dad's sudden departure, with no further contact, still brought pangs of anger and hurt to the surface. The distant relationship with my mom following my dad's leaving felt like a more subtle betrayal. I sat in my car, waiting for my wife to finish getting groceries. I should have gone in with her to help, but my mood was dark and silent. She did not ask me to go in with her.

I thought of my friend Carissa. The vision of her lifeless

body brought the same rumbling emotions of deep sadness and fear to the surface. The "then what" after death caused me to shudder. *What is the purpose of life, really? Why are we here? What really happens when we die?*

My heart rate seemed to grow forcibly and faster. Anxiety crept in like a prowling mountain lion, ready to pounce on my soul. I tried to pray, but my anger toward God, if there was one, kept me at bay. My talk with Marcus had opened a new window into my doubting soul. Still, the harsh realities of sudden tragedy and the loss of a father all those years ago caused the curtains to close quickly.

Suddenly, the hatch door opened, and my wife placed a couple of bags inside. Shutting the door, she walked around to the passenger side, opened the door, and silently entered. I started the engine, backed out of the parking spot, and headed home. I remained quiet.

As we pulled out onto the highway for the ten-minute drive home, Mary looked at me.

"Are you okay?" she asked.

"Yeah, I'm fine." I lied.

I could feel Mary's eyes staring at me in silence. Amid my doubts, I knew Mary's faith remained secure even during her battle with cancer. *Why couldn't I share her deep faith?*

We drove home in silence. After helping put the groceries away, I told Mary I needed to take a walk. I stepped out the front door into the cool autumn air and began walking. At the end of our street, a walking trail cut a path through the woods toward a small creek. I walked silently, still fuming from my memories. I realized my anger centered on my dad's sudden departure more than anything else. The feeling of abandonment and rejection pierced me deeply.

I walked alongside the creek now, the sound of the gurgling waters easing my pain. I listened to the crunching leaves and twigs under my feet, squirrels scurrying on the ground and in neighboring trees, and the ever-present sound of the creek. The combined sounds formed a gentle blanket to my aching soul, warming and embracing me with much-needed peace.

Suddenly, I stopped. A lone deer ahead stood drinking from the creek and quickly looked up at me. We both stared in silence for what seemed like minutes. The deer seemed to be sniffing the air, nervous and alert. Soon, it darted deeper into the woods, leaving me alone, mesmerized by its beauty and grace.

I wondered how much I was like that deer—nervous, fearful, ready to run from my fears and hurt at the slightest intrusion. I thought of my wife trying to get inside my head and heart. *Why am I so fearful of letting her in? Why do I run from her and others in my life?* I never talk with my brothers about the hurtful parts of our past. We all blissfully keep conversations on the surface, never venturing into the deep waters of our hurt and pain from our past with our parents. I don't dare broach the subject with my mom. She seems encased in a cocoon of denial and resistance.

I continued walking, deep in my thoughts. Returning depression and dread replaced the fleeting blanket of peace I felt a moment before. The pieces of the puzzle of my life remained a jumbled mess.

5

The Beauty Piece

The sun glared through my windshield as I neared the nursing home, causing me to squint. I observed birds and butterflies dancing in the air, singing and flapping their wings during their final joy before winter.

I pulled into the parking lot and got out of my car, noticing Marcus sitting again under the big maple tree, full of color. I decided my visit today would be with him first.

Marcus smiled as I approached. "Well, hello there, Mr. Wyatt! How are you this fine morning?"

"I'm well, Marcus. How are you?"

"Splendid! Enjoying the new day the Lord has given me!"

I admired how cheerful Marcus was while living in a nursing home with very few visitors other than myself and not even a trace of bitterness in his demeanor. I admired this new friend of mine.

I sat in an empty chair beside him, facing his maple, and stretched my legs out.

"How is your wife doing, Wyatt? Mary, right?"

"Yes, Mary. She's doing fine. Keeping busy teaching third graders."

Marcus chuckled. "I bet so. Those little ones will keep you on your toes!"

We sat in silence, both staring at a cardinal perched on a branch about ten feet from us. It was a bright-colored male.

As a lifelong St. Louis Cardinals baseball fan, I always enjoyed seeing their namesake. The warmth of the gentle autumn breeze amidst the changing color of leaves announcing the approaching winter brought a unique sweetness to the air.

"So, Wyatt, are we ready to talk about the next piece of my puzzle?" Marcus grinned as he spoke, reaching into his shirt pocket with another puzzle piece.

"How did you know I was coming today, Marcus?"

"I didn't. I just carry this piece around, reminding myself of this next puzzle piece. This discussion has been a good exercise for my faith, Wyatt. I want to thank you for sharing this gift with me."

"You're welcome, Marcus. Thank you for taking the time to have these discussions. They're giving me a lot to think about."

"Good!" Marcus said while patting my knee. "That's good!"

He turned the piece in his hand. "This piece we shall discuss today is beauty. Kind of fitting for us to talk about beauty while sitting outside looking at this here bird in this gorgeous maple, wouldn't you say?"

"Yes, pretty fitting," I said. "So, what does beauty have to do with why you believe in God?"

"Everything!" Marcus grinned. "Everything!"

"Okay." I laughed, tickled by his enthusiasm. "Explain."

"Oh, I will, my friend." Marcus chuckled. "Beauty is closely tied with the design piece. They fit together on the border of my puzzle of belief."

"How so?"

Marcus looked up toward the maple tree. "Remember me talking about how this tree has an obvious design and purpose? Within that design there is also beauty. Beauty is defined as a combination of qualities, such as shape, color, or form, that please the aesthetic senses, especially the sight. You see how that relates to design, Wyatt?"

I thought for a moment. "Yes, by that definition, the qualities of shape, color, and form all are products of design. Beauty then would be design that brings pleasure?"

"Exactly! Beauty is designed to bring us joy, lift our hearts, and give us hope and peace. Beauty is no accident, my friend!"

I looked closely at the tree, examining the many leaves and branches extending out. The fine detail of each leaf illustrated beauty and design, not random, mindless chance.

Marcus continued. "Think of what this world might look like if it were just randomly put together, rather than the product of an Intelligent Designer. How would it look?"

I thought about his question. "I'm not sure, Marcus. I guess it would be more chaotic and rugged. The point of evolution is survival of the fittest, so delicate items of creation would cease to exist by that definition.

"Such as flowers?" Marcus asked.

"Maybe so."

Marcus smiled. "It seems to me when we observe beauty in nature, it makes more sense that beauty is the product not of random chance, but of a God who loves beauty and who instilled it in creation."

We sat quietly for a moment, then Marcus continued.

"Also, why do we as humans appreciate beauty? Where did that come from? Why do we have artists who, through the centuries, have created masterful works of art in paintings, sculpture, and architecture? Where does that desire, creativity, and purpose come from? I suggest we appreciate and create beauty because we are made in God's image, who is the Creator of beauty."

I chuckled. "God sure didn't give me that gift!"

"Me either!" Marcus laughed. "Lord knows I can draw a mean stick figure, though!"

We both laughed, then sat in silence. I thought of my wife the first time I saw her. Her face glowed as she spoke. Her deep blue eyes stirred my soul and caused my heart rate to rise. Such beauty. My wife alone was an amazing work of art. I smiled.

Marcus looked at me. "What are you thinking about, Wyatt?" He winked.

"Just reflecting on beauty," I said.

Marcus chuckled. "Yes, sir, I bet you were! God's love and creativity is so evident in this world, isn't it?"

"Yes," I reluctantly agreed. "I guess so."

"For me, growing up in Arkansas," said Marcus, "I remember nights going outside and seeing the stars twinkling and dotting the sky as far as I could see. I would talk to God on those nights about whatever was on my mind. I remember after a good afternoon shower, seeing a rainbow with all its colors stretch from one end of the horizon to the other. I remember seeing similar colors in rainbow trout we pulled out of the river. I remember seeing my child being born and the first cries. Ten fingers and toes all perfectly formed."

Marcus grew silent, a sad look suddenly on his face.

"Are you okay?" I asked. I was concerned about him.

Marcus sighed. "Yes, Wyatt, I'm fine. Just reflecting."

I stared at Marcus. Pain etched deep grooves alongside the age spots on his face. I thought of probing further but decided to wait.

Marcus sighed but smiled. "These late fall days have some of the prettiest sunrises and sunsets. Bright reds and yellows painted across the horizon."

"Yes, this morning was like that," I said.

"It's done my heart good over the years to take long walks in the woods and simply notice the beauty," said Marcus. "If you look closely enough, it's everywhere. From the shape and color of rocks to the veins in maple leaves. So much variety and color and shapes of both living and non-living things. We take it for granted because it's all we know. I think that's why kids from the inner city are so amazed when they get out in the country. I've heard of kids growing up on the streets playing with leaves when they are at a park. They recognize beauty and are in awe."

"I've never thought of that," I said. "I guess I take beauty for granted in nature since this is all I've known."

"Me too, Wyatt. Growing up in Arkansas, I immersed myself in nature each day. I can still hear the quiet sounds of leaves crunching as I walked and the deep smell of the tall pines. Those quiet walks stilled my troubled soul many times over the years."

I drove home, reflecting on our conversation about beauty. I remembered my walks through the woods of the Ozark Mountains near my home. After a good rain, I would slowly make my way from our hilltop to the deep-cut valley with a flowing stream. I would hear the sound of birds singing to each other along the way, as my bruised heart cried for meaning and peace. The simple elegance and stillness of those moments brought me both wonder and hope amid anxiety and heartache with my family situation.

I walked into my house and saw my wife in the kitchen, apron on, fixing dinner. Her beauty seemed more pronounced after my conversation with Marcus. I embraced her, smelling her sweet fragrance and feeling the warmth of her body next to mine.

My Mary showed beauty deeply and brightly to my darkened soul. This piece of my puzzle made sense.

6

My Wife, Mary

It had been a long day. I sat in the break room at Walmart, nearing the end of my shift. My feet ached, and my voice grew shallow from dealing with customers and employees under me. I was ready to be done so I could go home and check on my wife.

Earlier in my life, I had dreamed of being a teacher and coach. The thought of molding young minds and influencing them toward a positive future excited me. However, after college finances were tight, and the Walmart store manager had already approached me about their manager training program. I decided being a teacher would have to wait if it ever were to happen at all.

Stuart Jones, a retired teacher who worked part-time, walked into the break room. It was just the two of us. I liked Stuart. He was friendly, positive, and caring. He was very good with customers. He spent part of his time as a greeter and, when needed, helped me in sporting goods. He seemed to be always available.

He looked at me as I sipped my coffee.

"How's it going, Wyatt?" he asked, patting me on my back as he sat beside me with his coffee.

"About ready to call it a day," I said, noticing how tired my voice was.

"Yep. Me too. Got plans for the evening?"

"Nope. Just going to watch TV with my wife and relax."

Stuart pulled up a little closer. "How is Mary?" I could see by the look on his face that he was concerned.

"She's doing okay. The chemo treatments really sap her energy."

Stuart nodded. "So sorry she's having to go through all of that."

I sighed. "Yeah, me too. She's tough, though. She'll get through this. We'll get through this."

"I know you will, Wyatt. But I'm sure it's got to be rough. I know when my Nancy had her stroke, those weeks in the hospital drained me, along with the loneliness at home."

"I didn't know about your wife. How long ago was that?"

"About three years ago. She's doing much better today. Only walks with a slight limp but does use a cane. Her speech is back to normal too!"

I smiled. "Good! How long have the two of you been married now?"

Stuart didn't hesitate. "Fifty-four years this next April. We've kind of gotten used to each other!" He chuckled.

"That's great, Stuart. I'm hoping Mary and I will be able to celebrate fifty-four years as well." I looked down and sighed.

Stuart patted me on the back again. "I'm praying for you both, Wyatt. I'm sure Mary will lick this cancer, and you two will have kids and grandkids someday!" He smiled and walked out of the breakroom.

Alone now, I thought about Mary. We just found out two months before of her rare form of cancer. It was in her lungs and liver and had already spread to her lymph nodes in several places. The oncologist we met with said that with aggressive chemo treatments and potential radiation, her cancer could be beaten, at least for now. She said the chances of its return, if put into remission, were over 50 percent.

We were just getting ready to try and get pregnant with our first child. Mary had suffered two miscarriages, and after the second one, we waited almost a year to try again. Now this. I sighed again, reflecting on my recent conversation with Marcus about beauty as a piece of the puzzle for God's existence. I hadn't told Marcus yet about Mary's situation. I was having a difficult time seeing true beauty while my wife suffered.

I had met Mary at a small diner where she was my waitress. I came in by myself for breakfast that day before heading to work. I remember her kind voice and gentle, shy smile. I was smitten from the start. I asked her out as I got up to leave. She smiled shyly and gave me her number.

On our first date, we went to a park and had a picnic, getting to know each other and slowly brushing off the awkwardness. I recall shaking my head in wonder, deeply impressed with Mary's sincere faith, love for children, and compassion toward people. In my mind, all the boxes were being checked off concerning what I wanted in a wife—all this on our first date!

We married only six months afterwards. We have now been married for five years. We are still without children, and my sweet Mary is fighting for her life.

I see no beauty in that.

I drove into my driveway from work just after six p.m., weary of being around people and ready to spend a quiet evening with Mary. When I got inside I called for her.

Mary came out of the kitchen, smiling and greeting me with a kiss and hug. Even in her suffering, the same kindness, compassion, and love emanated. I held her longer than usual, tears welling up. I said a quick, silent, and pointed prayer. "Lord, heal her."

I know it's ironic that I prayed to a God I wasn't sure I believed existed. Were fear and desperation causing me to pray just in case God was real? I do not know. The conversation about design with Marcus caused my mind and heart to spin in a shaky cycle like an old washing machine. Anger mixed with the wash. *What did Mary do to deserve this suffering? How could I go on with life without her?*

Mary pulled back and looked at me. "Are you okay, honey?"

"Yes, I'm okay." I lied. "How are you?"

"I'm feeling pretty good today," she said, smiling, though her eyes spoke differently. They looked tired and worn.

"How was work?" she asked. I could tell she wanted to change the subject.

"It was fine. Not too busy a day."

Mary kissed me. "Well, dinner is almost ready. Why don't you get cleaned up, and I'll set the table."

I watched Mary walk back into the kitchen. Tears of fear and anger welled up again, and near panic set a firm grip on my heart. I quickly walked into the bathroom and closed the door. I stared at the mirror and whispered a prayer again to a mysterious God.

7

Fine-Tuning Piece

I sat by my grandmother's bed. She looked tired but was smiling. Her long hair was white, and her eyes echoed hollow reminders of the younger woman I knew as a child, though the spark still showed.

"How are you feeling, Grandma?" I asked, holding her hand.

"I'm okay, Wyatt," she replied, still smiling. "I need to get out of bed more, though. Getting lazy!" She chuckled.

"Let's do something about that!" I quickly jumped up and asked for a nurse.

A nurse came back in a few minutes with a wheelchair, and with my help, we got Grandma situated. I whisked her out of her room and decided to take her over to see Marcus.

Marcus was at his table working on his puzzle. I could see he had made progress, but hundreds of pieces lay still without a home. He smiled when he saw me approach, pushing Grandma.

"Well, look at that beautiful lady coming my way!" Marcus said.

"And look at that handsome man!" Grandma Mabel said.

Marcus reached his hand and grabbed Mabel's. The two smiled at each other and held hands for a moment.

"Hello, Marcus," I interrupted, happy to have these two together.

"Hello there, Wyatt. How are you today?"

"I'm doing well overall. Hope you don't mind me bringing my grandma to join us today."

"Not at all! Not at all," Marcus said, looking at Grandma. "It's always a pleasure to be in the company of dear Miss Mabel!"

"Oh, listen to yourself!" Grandma said, laughing. "You are always the charmer!"

"You bring it out of me, sweet lady," Marcus said, grabbing her hand again.

We sat and chit-chatted for a while, enjoying the warmth of the sun shining through the large window nearby.

Marcus suddenly picked up one of the pieces on the table and looked directly at me.

"Son, let's talk about another reason I believe there's a God who is alive and loves us!"

I smiled. "Okay, let's do it! You want to hear this, Grandma?"

"I most certainly do! I love talking about what truly matters."

"As do I, sweet lady," Marcus said, nodding. "As do I."

Marcus held the piece up. "This piece I like to call fine-tuning. Wyatt, do you play any musical instruments?"

"Yes, I have a guitar that I play. Not great, but I can play some notes."

"Do you know how to tune your guitar?" Marcus asked, still holding up the puzzle piece.

"Yes, I use a guitar tuner app from my phone."

"Good. So, the guitar tuner fine tunes your guitar to produce the right sound, correct?"

"Yes, that's correct."

Marcus smiled, setting the piece back on the table. "Just as your tuner helps give your guitar the proper sound, there are many, many things that had to take place to fine tune this universe so you and I could be here. So many different things that it is logical to believe that there must be a master tuner out there who fine-tuned the universe to make all of this happen!"

"What sort of things?"

"Good question!" Marcus said, leaning forward. "Many researchers point out over thirty specific areas of fine-tuning that have to be perfectly balanced for sustainable life to exist here on earth. Let's just look at a few."

Marcus pointed to the ground. "If I could get up out of this wheelchair and jump in the air, what keeps me from floating off into space?"

"Gravity," Grandma said quickly, smiling.

"Good! That's right sweet Mabel!" Marcus laughed. "Gravity holds us all on this planet. But did you know that the force of gravity must be a precise amount for us to even be alive? A slight increase relative to the universe in gravity on our planet would crush any animal larger than an insect!"

"Wow," I said. "And I assume if gravity was any less, we would all float off into space like balloons!"

Grandma and Marcus both laughed, looking up at me. "That would be quite the sight!" Grandma said.

Marcus folded his arms. "There are many other factors in the universe and our world that have to be extremely precise for life to be possible. Our earth is exactly the right distance from our sun. If we were just a little further away, the planet would be too cold for stable water cycles. Water is life. If our earth were a little closer, it would be too warm for stable water cycles. The tilt of our earth is just right. Because of the precise tilt, we have moderate temperatures necessary for life to exist. Any change in the tilt by even a fraction of a degree would be catastrophic."

Marcus looked at me. "What do you think about that, Wyatt?"

"Very interesting. I wonder, though, since there are billions of galaxies and billions and billions of stars in our universe, just by chance, could not these factors have all come together?"

Marcus smiled. "Sure, I suppose, if these items I mentioned were all the factors. But there are many more!"

"Such as?" I asked.

"Well . . . let's see. The rotation period for our planet to rotate around the sun is just right for life to exist. The thickness of our earth's crust is just right for life. If it were any thicker, too much oxygen would escape from the atmosphere to the crust. Any thinner, then volcanic and earthquake activity would tear the world apart. The planet Jupiter is just the right size and distance from our planet. It takes the hit time and time again from asteroids and comets that would otherwise destroy our planet. Even the size and shape of our Milky Way galaxy is necessary for life to be possible."

Marcus continued. "Another example of fine tuning goes way down into each atom in the universe. If you change the difference between a strong and weak nuclear force, even a small fraction between neutrons and protons, nuclear fusion in stars would cease. From this, there would be no energy source for life."

"My, Marcus, I didn't know you knew so much!" Grandma said, her eyes shining.

Marcus chuckled. "Oh, Miss Mable. I've just read a lot of books and magazine articles in my day. I've learned from lots of way smarter people than me. Without the fine-tuning of many contingent factors, life would be impossible in the universe. On the other hand, a random, purposeless universe would be life-prohibiting."

Looking at me, Marcus pointed out the window up to the sky. "Taking these examples of fine-tuning, and many more I've not mentioned, many scientists say the statistical probability of all of this happening by chance is so small it's ridiculous. Just looking at one example, the cosmological constant, is enough to boggle the mind."

"What is the cosmological constant?" I asked.

"Well, now. Let's see. It's part of Einstein's equation for general relativity. A simple way to explain it would be the energy density of empty space. Because of its force, it prevents matter from clumping together in the early universe, the process that helped form galaxies, stars, and you and me. Without this force the universe, instead of expanding as it is doing, would collapse instead into itself. Not good for you and me," Marcus said.

"So, is the cosmological constant fine-tuned?" I asked.

Marcus smiled. "Very precisely! Dr. Robin Collins, who is way smarter than me, said the fine-tuning of the cosmological constant is one part in ten followed by fifty-three zeroes! That's a number I cannot even say! He gave an illustration of this number. He said if you were way out in space and were going to throw a dart at random toward earth, it would be like hitting a bull's eye on earth that's one trillionth of a trillionth of an inch in diameter. That's smaller than the size of an atom!"

"Wow. That's unbelievable!" I said, blown away by this illustration.

"It is unbelievable, Wyatt, if you take God out of the equation," Marcus said. "Let's say I have a coin, and I bet you a hundred dollars that I could toss it in the air one hundred times in a row and have it land on heads every time. If that happens, will you think that's chance or that I have a rigged coin?"

"Rigged for sure," I said.

"Correct. Now take that times a billion. That's not even getting close to the chance of all this fine-tuning for life on this planet being from chance."

I sat there stunned. This piece of the puzzle, fine-tuning for life, was amazing. Marcus just smiled at me, and Grandma hummed an old hymn.

8

Moral Code Piece

Two weeks had passed since my last visit to Grandma and Marcus. It still hung in my thoughts, gnawing at my doubts while sprouting tiny mustard seeds of hope. Yet my past and present circumstances allowed little watering of those seeds. Seeing my wife the night before, sick and weak from her chemo treatments, shot renewed anger and doubts in my soul. As if God really exists, I told myself as I drove. He must be distant and uncaring. He shows no real character that I can see.

After a brief visit with Grandma, who dozed in and out, I returned to the big room to see Marcus, who sat in his usual spot with his puzzle.

"Hello, Marcus. Good to see you," I said.

"Well, look who's here!" Marcus smiled and extended his hand. "How are you today, Mr. Wyatt?"

I grasped Marcus' hand and returned his smile. "I'm doing okay. Our last talk on the fine-tuning for life has been on my mind a lot the past two weeks. You made some interesting points."

"Well now. In my puzzle of belief, I like to use fine-tuning as one of my corner pieces. It helps build the framework for reality for sure."

"Do you have a puzzle piece for me today?"

"Yes, sir, I do!" Marcus laughed.

He motioned for me to sit down, which I did.

Marcus picked up what looked like another corner piece. "This piece here I call the moral law. Do you know what the moral law is, Wyatt?"

"Umm, I'm not sure. It sounds like it has to do with the idea of right and wrong?"

"Exactly!" Marcus said, smiling and shaking the piece in his hand. "The idea of right and wrong—where did that come from?"

I thought for a moment. "Good question. If you believe in God, I will say from Him. If you don't, I guess it has come about as a way of survival."

"Yes, I think that's an astute observation," Marcus said. "This idea of right and wrong, if you read any kind of book—whether fiction, non-fiction, biography, or history—all have elements of this concept all through time. Why is that?"

"Good question. I'm not sure."

Marcus leaned forward toward me. "Think about it, Wyatt. Every culture in the world, from the most civilized to those in remote places, understands basic moral principles, such as kindness and love, and evil and murder. Where does that come from?"

I sat back in my chair. I remember as a young boy knowing that how my parents interacted was wrong and how I treated my siblings was wrong. I also remember feeling a deep sense of joy and rightness when I helped a classmate who fell off the monkey bars or helped my mom clean the kitchen. *Where did that sense of right and wrong come from in my life?*

Marcus smiled at me. "Wyatt, I believe in my heart this sense of right and wrong, the moral law, did not come about through evolution, but from a Creator who wrote that law on our hearts from the beginning of time."

"But what about horrible events in our history like the Holocaust and slavery?" I asked. "How does that line up with a moral law within us? What happened to the sense of right and wrong?'

Marcus nodded. "Yes, slavery, the Holocaust, and all the innocent little lives taken by abortion are all examples of man ignoring the moral law. But think about it, Wyatt, you bringing those examples up is because you know they are very wrong, correct? How do you know they are wrong?"

"I guess I know they are wrong because of the moral law."

"Exactly. The sad fact is because of sin and this broken world, man chooses to ignore the moral law for various reasons, mostly selfish ones. The more we ignore the moral law, the harder our hearts become to it. This is the work of the evil one."

Marcus suddenly had a faraway look in his eyes. His smile faded.

"What's wrong, Marcus?" I asked.

He sighed. "Just remembering, Wyatt. I was a broken man about your age or maybe a little younger. I ignored the moral law because I had been hurt bad and was angry at people . . . and God."

"Do you mind telling me about it?"

Marcus let out another deep sigh, looking out the big window and folding his arms.

"Well, now, where do I begin? I guess you could say my pain started as a boy. We lived in southern Arkansas in a small town. My daddy was an alcoholic who was an angry drunk. He would beat me and my three brothers often, and while never hitting Mama, would say terrible things to her. It was a scary time when he would come home from his job in construction drunk."

Marcus shook his head. I noticed a small tear rolling down his cheek.

"I'm so sorry, Marcus," I said.

"Yep. But I tell you, my mama was a saint. Through it all she managed to take us boys to church every Sunday. Dad never joined us. He was angry at God for the racism he dealt with all his life. When we were little, Mom would come to our bedsides every night and pray for us. In her I saw Christ for the first time."

Marcus shifted in his chair. "When I got older and graduated high school, I wanted to go to college to study to be a teacher. I had a couple of teachers in high school, including my baseball coach, who impacted my life in a positive way. I thought I could influence young minds too. But college was expensive even back then, and honestly was hard to get in if you were a black person, so after high school I started working with my dad and older brothers in construction. By then my brothers all drank too. I never drank. I never wanted to be like my dad."

I could see the pain in Marcus' eyes as he spoke.

"I worked with my dad and brothers for about a year. That was the hardest year of my life. I was lonely, angry and saw no future for my life. I felt trapped. I also saw lots of racism where I worked. Not from everyone, but from several. I saw it at the grocery store with the manager always keeping a close eye on me when I shopped. I saw it with the police. I got pulled over several times for no apparent reason. It further increased the darkness in my heart."

"Wow, I'm sorry Marcus," I said, shaking my head.

"I grew angry with God, wondering if He was such a God of love and mercy, why had He forgotten to give me any of it.

I grew bitter and doubtful that God even existed. Finally, I started to drink with my brothers and Dad. I ended up being pulled over for a DWI and lost my license for a year."

Marcus shook his head. "I was so dumb. I knew in my heart God was real, but anger and bitterness put a dark cloud over me, casting a deep separation from God. That year without a license I grew depressed. I felt worthless, like a failure. Finally, one night I decided to take my life, but God had other plans."

Marcus shifted again in his seat. Another tear slowly ran its path down his cheek. I wanted to say something to encourage him but could only lean forward and listen.

"I went for a walk down into the woods near our home. I had taken my father's gun with a single bullet. I wanted to go deep into the woods, alone, to end my pain. As I walked, I started thinking about life and all my hurt. I reflected on all the racial slurs, all the hatred and anger—all the abuse from my father, both verbal and physical. My heart was so heavy, Wyatt."

Marcus sighed, then smiled. "But then, as I sat under a large oak tree, ready to pull the gun from my pants pocket, I saw a mother deer and a fawn, probably only fifty feet from me. I sat in silence, and the two started walking right toward me. I could tell they saw me, but for some reason, they didn't seem afraid. I'm not lying to you, Wyatt. That mother deer and her fawn walked right up to me. I sat there, stunned and frozen as both deer licked my forehead, face, and the hand that was about to pull out the gun to end my life."

"Wow," I whispered.

"Yes, wow!" Marcus said, shaking his head. "I began to weep, and the two deer trotted off quietly. I knew right then and there that God was saying to me He loved me and would never leave or forsake me. Through His creation He reached out to me in a powerful way. I've never been the same since."

We both sat silently for a time, reflecting on the incredible miracle. Just then, we both gasped at the same time. A doe slowly walked up near the large maple tree and stared at us.

Marcus chuckled.

I just stared with my mouth open.

I sat in my recliner later that evening alone. Mary had gone to bed early. I reflected on my time with Marcus and the strange coincidence of the deer appearing just after Marcus told me the story of the deer saving his life. *Was this just a coincidence? Or did God show up, using the deer to both encourage Marcus and show me in a tangible, physical way He was there with us?*

I sighed. I truly wanted to believe in a God of love and compassion who always leans into our lives. Instead, looking back over my past and peering at the present, all I could see were large pockets of a God of silence and hiding. Why doesn't God show up every day as it appeared He had today? Why does He often choose to be hidden and silent?

I struggled to sleep that night. I wanted this puzzle piece to fit into my life, but the jagged edges of hurt resisted.

9

College Years

I remember my time at Central Missouri State University. Thinking back to my college years brought back pleasant as well as harsh memories.

One in particular stands out. Her name was Chris. From a northern suburb of Chicago, she was tall, brown-haired, and very smart. Chris and I met as fellow resident assistants in adjacent dorms on campus. She kept smiling at me when we talked, and my heartbeat quickened. We started hanging out together during our free time, going on walks and talking in each other's rooms.

I fell hard.

We went to church together and began holding hands as we walked. She wanted to pursue a counseling career. I wanted to be in sports broadcasting or a teacher and coach. We both talked about being missionaries, too, with thoughts of doing that together.

I woke up each morning thinking of Chris, anxious to see her and hear her voice and laughter. I remember it was fall, approaching Thanksgiving break. I deliberated about asking her to come home with me to meet my family.

I attended and helped lead the Fellowship of Christian Athletes on campus. Chris participated in the Baptist Student Union. Between this, our roles as resident assistants, and class schedules, we had to fight for quality time together. I began noticing a strain with Chris when we met. Her smiles became less, and her joy seemed to slip. She shared she dealt with anxiety and depression, and lately, she struggled to get up in the morning.

About a week before Thanksgiving break, she called and asked if we could meet in her room. She didn't sound good.

I walked into her room. She sat on her bed, crying.

"What's wrong, Chris?" I asked, putting my arm around her and sitting next to her.

She did not answer with words. She put her head on my shoulder and sighed. I could feel her tears drip off her cheek onto my arm. I chose to remain silent with her for a time and simply hold her.

Suddenly she lifted up her head and looked me in the eyes.

"I hate to do this to you. I really love you, Wyatt. But I can't love you."

A hard, sharp pain settled on my chest. My throat tightened.

"What do you mean?" I said, trying to find meaning in her eyes.

She began to cry. Covering her face with her hands, she put her elbows on her knees. I rubbed her back and waited.

After about a minute, she leaned back, took a deep breath, and looked at me again. Her makeup had become smeared on her face.

"I can't really explain, Wyatt. It's not you. Not you at all. I'm just not in a healthy place for a relationship."

I remember placing my hands on her shoulders, looking into her eyes, and telling her I would give her space but would remain her friend.

I left her room heartbroken, but the real pain began in the days ahead. When I tried to reach out to her to see how she was doing, she did not respond. She didn't answer my calls. I felt utterly rejected.

I remember going home to see my family for Thanksgiving break alone. I tried to cover my pain with my family, not sharing about my relationship breakup. Finally, the pain became so intense I had to get away alone. I took a long walk on my parents' land in the woods and yelled at God. "Why did you let this happen, Lord? I thought she was the one!"

My words echoed into the distant hills. The silence enfolded me as my deep pain remained. Until Christmas break, I struggled deeply with not seeing or hearing from Chris. Finally, I gave up trying and attempted to move on, heavy-hearted and lonely.

I sat on my couch now, ruminating on those memories while staring at my wife asleep next to me in the recliner, a blanket pulled up to her chin. Marcus and his story of pain, racism, and rejection brought back my own darkened memories. From a distant father to a love of my life abandoning me suddenly, to a dear wife fighting for her life, filtering all that pain with the picture of a God of love and compassion proved frustrating and confusing.

I sighed. Another visit with Grandmother was coming in a couple of days, and hopefully another talk with Marcus. I enjoyed my visits with him, but this last one brought back old wounds for both of us.

I stared at my wife. "Lord, please don't take Mary from me. I'm not sure I could handle another loss."

The thought of losing Mary brought a sense of sudden panic to my heart. I imagined life without her, alone in this house, the smell of her hair and the sound of her sweet voice gone forever. A tear suddenly escaped my eye. In all my pain and life's seeming unfairness, Mary brought renewed joy. She loved me unconditionally, cared for others consistently, and believed in God and His love. Even now, while I battled my faith, she remained firmly devoted to me. In my heart, I knew I was a fortunate man.

I thought of Chris again, wondering where she was now and how she was doing. I said a quick prayer for her as well. It intrigued me that, while questioning if there really is a God, lately, it seemed I talked to Him an awful lot. What's happening to me?

10

Story Piece

I got permission to take Marcus for a drive.

Marcus grinned as we drove. "I can't tell you when the last time I've been in a car, Wyatt," he said. "Must have been on my kids' visit last Christmas. They took me to a nice restaurant, and I had a big juicy steak!"

We drove down toward Table Rock Lake. It was now early spring, and the weather was warmer than usual for March. I parked near a pavilion overlooking the lake. I helped Marcus out of the car then pulled two comfortable outdoor chairs out of the trunk. We found a nice spot under a large oak tree with a pristine view of the quiet waters.

"Wow! This is gorgeous!" Marcus said as he scanned the view. "I really appreciate you taking the time to bring me here, Wyatt. What a blessing!"

"It's my pleasure, Marcus. I thought it would be good for you to get away from your home for a while and enjoy this beautiful day."

Leaves were starting to bud from their winter slumber, and birds were singing all around, celebrating the day's warmth. I scanned the lake and noticed a lone fishing boat in a cove. Two fishermen were standing and casting their reels.

Marcus smiled and sighed, leaning back in his chair. "As a boy, I remember fishing with my brothers. We used homemade cane poles on a creek near our home. Caught lots of catfish!"

I sighed. My dad rarely took me fishing growing up, and even when he did, once we got to the spot, he would silently walk away to his own area, leaving us to fend for ourselves.

Marcus didn't notice my distraction. He was busy staring at the lake and smiling.

"I forgot to bring a piece from my puzzle, but I do have another reason I believe in God I'd like to discuss with you, Wyatt."

I broke from my thoughts and turned to my friend. "Oh, what piece might that be?"

"Story."

"Story? What about story?"

"Well, sir," Marcus said as he leaned forward with his elbows resting on his knees, "story shows us that a writer beyond our understanding of time invented the concept of story."

"I'm not sure I follow."

Marcus turned to me. "Think about it, Wyatt. Let's just think about our favorite movies. What are some of your all-time favorites?"

"I've always enjoyed movies. I love the *Lord of the Rings* trilogy and *Star Wars*. I also like the Jason Bourne movies."

"Good. I guess my taste goes further back! I loved *In the Heat of the Night* with Sidney Poitier. He was fantastic! I also loved *Glory* and *Shawshank Redemption*."

Marcus tapped my knee. "Now tell me, what made the movies you loved so good?"

I thought for a minute. "As I think about it, in all my movies there was a battle or conflict between good characters and bad ones. Also, a lot of good action!"

Marcus chuckled. "Yes, indeed. You hit on something there. Good characters versus bad characters. How do you know who is good and who is bad?"

I frowned. "That's a good question, Marcus. In old westerns, the bad characters wore black cowboy hats, and the good guys wore white. It's a bit more complex now. I guess the bad characters do evil things, like Darth Vader. Come to think of it, he was dressed in black as well!"

I smiled.

Marcus persisted. "But how do you know what they are doing is evil?"

I smiled. "I guess it goes back to the moral code?"

"Exactly. The moral code is woven into all good stories. And as I've said before, the moral code points to the One who made it."

"Hmm. Interesting."

I sighed, letting Marcus' words sink in. A bald eagle suddenly flew out of a distant tree on the other side of the lake and across the waters. Marcus and I both watched in silent admiration.

Marcus resumed. "Story involves elements or pieces of life that point to a larger story. The story of God and His relationship to us, His creation, is described in the Bible. All good stories that touch our hearts hearken back to God's grander and greater story."

"It seems a stretch to me to say that story proves there is a God," I said, folding my arms as I stretched my legs. "I mean, can't story just evolve as part of man's experience?"

"Well now, I'm not saying this idea of story pointing to God proves He's God, Wyatt. Remember, this is just one piece of many for me. You are correct, it doesn't prove anything. To me, though, it begs the question: Why does a good story always have this idea of good and evil or overcoming a problem? Why does that appeal to us?"

I thought about his question for a moment. "Maybe it appeals to us because we put ourselves in the story and want to overcome, to succeed."

Marcus leaned forward. "If there is no God and when we die, we simply cease to exist, what is the point of overcoming, of succeeding, if it ends in nothing? I think written into all our lives, our stories, is this longing for something outside of this life, a bigger story. Otherwise, all is pointless."

I sat in silence. The thought of there being no God suddenly hit me with all its implications. If there is no God, then success means nothing. Life means nothing. If our universe and each of us are merely traveling aimlessly toward utter extinction, then what's really the point? The thought caused my heart to despair.

Marcus noticed my frown. "What's the matter, Wyatt?"

I hesitated. "Well . . . it just occurred to me that if there is no God, then all our stories are pointless. And the moral code is also pointless."

Marcus nodded. "True. If there is no God and when we die, we just cease to exist, then there truly is no hope. And that's a scary thought if you do not believe."

"So, what is the importance of my story if God's story is really what matters?"

Marcus smiled. "Well, Wyatt, each of our stories matter so greatly to God. You see, His story interweaves each of our stories as part of His story. He is writing His wonderful story of love, restoration, and fulfillment through our stories. The good, the bad and the uncertain. I believe He uses them all in a mysterious way."

"So, our stories matter?" My words came out in a whisper as my sudden emotion surprised me.

Marcus put a hand on my knee as he leaned toward me.

"Oh yes, Wyatt. Our stories, when surrendered to God's bigger story, will reverberate forever. Our stories are a big part of His story!"

We drove back in silence, each deep in thought. The idea of story pointing to the truth of God's existence and relationship with each of us had never occurred to me. I thought about all the childhood stories read to me and the movies I enjoyed through the years. All stories either gave hope or showcased a fallen world, or both. It made sense that this idea of a "good" story seemed consistent and connected. Thinking again of the biblical story of God as creator, sustainer, and in Jesus, savior, I felt tears forming in my eyes reflecting on this much more powerful and grander story.

How was my story fitting into God's story? I wasn't sure, but I wanted to investigate further. In the depths of my mind, I could almost hear a couple of pieces clicking together.

11

My Sister, Sharon

I stared at the casket, laden with flowers, a mixture of roses and daisies, her favorites. Family and friends gazed with me as a minister spoke, his words drowned out by my grief and anger.

Sharon's body lay inside that casket. My sister.

She died at eighteen, a product of depression and grief brought on by a hidden abuse we knew nothing about until shortly before her suicide.

The abuse occurred while on a mission trip with our church. Sharon, fifteen at the time, loved helping people. While quiet, her heart burst with joy when she served others, especially those less fortunate. On a particular mission trip, one of the male chaperones molested her. She spoke to nobody about this, but after her return, she seemed anxious, distracted, and sullen.

Before long, she no longer wanted to attend youth group. She spent most evenings alone in her room. Sharon finally told her loving youth minister and his wife what had happened. The arrest and trial brought more grief, more stress, and lackluster support from our mom.

My sister's heart shattered.

With her suicide, my faith went too.

Why would God allow this horrible thing to happen? On a mission trip of all places? I grew angry with God in the weeks following her death, then distant, bitter, and hollowed out. My mom would not talk about Sharon following her death. Dad was out of the picture. My mom turned to alcohol and television, rarely leaving the house. My visits became more and more infrequent. I saw Sharon's sad eyes each time I looked at my mom.

It was too much.

I sighed, sitting by Grandma's bedside as she slept, reflecting on the horrible event just three years ago. It broke Grandma's heart and seemed to speed her decline. My faith also crumbled with Sharon's death. She loved God and served Him, and this was His response?

I shook my head. I missed my sister.

Grandma stirred and looked at me.

"Wyatt, is that you, or am I dreaming?"

"It's me, Grandma." I put my hand on hers.

"You look sad, Wyatt. What's wrong?"

"Oh, nothing, Grandma. Just waiting for you to wake up. How are you feeling?"

Grandma stared at me. "I'm fine, but I don't think you are, young man. I may be old and dying, but I still know my grandson. Tell me what's bothering you."

I sighed. Grief hung like a thick blanket.

"I miss Sharon, Grandma."

Grandma nodded slowly. "I know, hon. I miss her too but am excited that I will see her soon."

"How can you be so sure, Grandma?" My doubts burst from my sorrow-laden heart.

Grandma stared at me for a moment and smiled. "I know because lately I have felt her presence, Wyatt. I know because I know my Lord, and I know Sharon. She was a kind but wounded soul. She suffers no more and is waiting for our reunion . . . as am I."

Grandma's eyes brimmed with tears through her smile. I admired her firm and constant faith, even during her own suffering.

Grandma suddenly chuckled. "I remember Sharon and you coming over to see me and wanting to play hide and seek! You were a good hider, but Sharon wasn't so good! She would hide just a few feet from where I counted. She never liked being too far from me."

"She sure loved you, Grandma. She loved being with you."

Grandma smiled. "And we will be together again soon. I can't wait!"

Grandma's eyes closed. I knew it was time to let her sleep. I decided to go visit Marcus for a bit before heading home.

Marcus was once again working on his puzzle. He smiled as I approached.

"Well, hello there, Wyatt! So good to see you, my friend!"

"Hello, Marcus! How is the puzzle coming?

"Well . . . slow but sure. Got the border done and now working toward the middle. How is sweet Mable doing?"

I sat down next to Marcus. "She is asleep now. Her heart is doing well. Her body seems to be tiring easier."

"Sweet Mable. Always a smile and a kind word from her. I'll miss her when she graduates."

"Graduates? You mean dies? That's an interesting way of putting it."

Marcus set his puzzle piece down. "When you believe in life eternal, it truly is a graduation when you pass from this life to forever life. I know Miss Mable will graduate to eternity with Jesus."

I nodded. "If indeed there is life after this, my grandma will be there. I do not know anyone with more faith than her."

Marcus looked directly at me. "If you don't mind me asking, Wyatt, what did you and your grandmother talk about today? You seem a little distracted."

I hesitated. "We talked about my sister, Sharon, and her passing, and some nice memories of her."

"I see," Marcus said, looking down. "So sorry to hear of your sister's passing. How long ago did this happen?"

"About three years ago."

Marcus didn't pry. He simply put a hand on my knee. "Losing those we love brings the most pain in life. I remember when my brother, Kiel, was murdered."

"Murdered?"

Marcus sighed. "Yes. He was shot in a drive-by shooting in Little Rock. Random, stupid, and pointless." Marcus frowned, shaking his head.

"I'm so sorry, Marcus. Such a tragedy."

"Yes, Wyatt, like your sister's death sounds like a tragedy. In this fallen, broken world, nobody is immune from unfair and horrible things. The Bible says the rain will fall on the righteous and the unrighteous. None of us is immune no matter how close we are to God."

I shook my head. "This is one of the reasons I'm having trouble believing in God, Marcus. That just doesn't seem fair."

Marcus looked at me again. "To quote author Philip Yancey, 'Life is unfair. God is fair. Don't confuse the two.' We live in a broken world because we have left God and gone our own way—all of us. The result is a dangerous, unpredictable, fallen world. God is holy and just, but He also has given us free will. It's part of the mystery of my puzzle of why I believe that still doesn't completely fit, but as I'm getting closer to graduating from this life, the picture is getting clearer."

"How so?" I really wanted to know.

"Well, the more I observe this world, from all my memories of racism and hatred to tough relationships with family, to wars and poverty, I believe there is evil. But the more I observe the good things, from the beauty of creation, to acts of kindness and compassion, the more I believe there is goodness and love in the world too. As I contrast good and evil, the truth of the Bible rings truer and truer, and the truth of God's voice in my heart rings truer and truer."

Marcus smiled. A single tear was trickling down his cheek. I didn't know what to say.

Marcus patted my knee. "I pray for you daily, Wyatt. You have become very special to me in our short time together. Thank you for sharing with me about losing your sister. It helps me pray more specifically for you."

Tears welled up in my eyes. The kindness and compassion shown by Marcus surprised me since I rarely experienced it growing up. I felt grateful to receive it daily from my wife, but this unexpected gift from my new friend, a black man I didn't know until recently, moved me deeply.

"Thank you," I managed to say through my tears.

Driving home, I sensed the thick blanket of grief changing to a lighter, cooler blanket. Love from my grandma and friend had been a balm to my wounds. Tiny sprouts of hope seemed to be growing somewhere deep in my soul, and another piece of my puzzle seemed to click in place. I wasn't sure how, but the picture was slowly coming together.

12

Learning About Grandma

Grandma Mable smiled as I wheeled her outside. The early May sun smiled on us as I rolled her down the walkway. The birds sang songs of joy, and the fresh-cut grass invigorated my senses. We stopped at the tree Marcus loved. I pulled up a chair by Grandma to enjoy the warmth and beauty of the day.

"Thank you, Wyatt, for visiting me so often. I always look forward to seeing you!" She reached her shaking hand toward mine. I held it and smiled at her.

"You are more than welcome, Grandma. I look forward to our visits as well!"

I held her hand as we sat in silence, listening to nature welcome us to their home. Our hearts warmed to the songs of birds, the buzzing of bees, and the whisper of the warm breeze on our faces.

Grandma shook her head gently, still smiling.

"God sure has outdone Himself today, Wyatt!"

I smiled back. "Yes, it is a gorgeous day for sure."

Grandma tightened her grip on my hand. "Wyatt, how are you doing, really?"

I hesitated. "I'm doing okay, Grandma. You don't have to worry about me."

"Okay. How is Mary?"

Grandma always talked directly. That's part of what I love about her.

"She's hanging in there, Grandma. The cancer treatments leave her very weak, but she's in good spirits. The doctors feel good about her progress."

"That's good. That's good," Grandma said, searching my eyes. "I pray for you both every day, you know."

"I know, Grandma. I sure appreciate it."

We sat in silence for a time, alone in our thoughts. I decided to change the subject.

"Tell me what it was like for you as a kid, Grandma. Where again did you live?"

Grandma chuckled. "Oh my, that was so long ago! Of course, I do remember, though!" She patted my hand. "I grew up over in Barry County on a farm not too far from Wheatland. My mom and dad raised me and my two older brothers back during the tail end of the depression. Those were hard times, Wyatt."

"I bet. Was it a happy childhood?"

She smiled. "Oh yes! We didn't know we were poor back then. We just lived each day, worked hard, played hard, and fought hard!" She laughed.

"I remember my brothers picked on me a lot. They would throw acorn shells at me. Never really hurt—just got on my nerves. They were good to me as well. Taught me how to catch catfish with a cane pole, gig frogs from the pond, and shoot a rabbit or squirrel."

"You shot rabbits and squirrels?" I was shocked.

"Oh yeah. I think I was a better shot than my brothers!" She winked.

It was great seeing Grandma laughing and recalling good memories. I could tell this time meant a lot to her. I looked at her, admiring her strength, joy, and faith. I know she had not had an easy life. Grandpa, while faithful to her as far as I know, wasn't always kind. He had a temper and bossed her around a lot. She always took his tantrums in stride, while giving it back too!

"I remember the winter of 1940, I believe. I would have been about eight years old then." Grandma's eyes narrowed as she thought. "That was a cold winter, Wyatt. I can still feel the chill in my bones. We must have had three feet of snow that winter, and the wind seemed to blow nonstop for the whole months of January and February. I helped my pappy break the ice on our pond every morning. He broke the ice and I watched." She smiled.

"Where were your brothers?" I asked.

"Oh, they helped feed the cattle straw and chopped lots of firewood. We had a potbelly stove in the center of our living room. When it got really cold, we pulled our mattresses down by the fire and slept."

"You mean you and your brothers?"

"No. All of us. Pappy and Momma too!"

I smiled, looking at Grandma, her eyes still bright and alive as she recalled these memories. I tried to picture her as a young girl, full of life with hopes and dreams. I imagined her in pigtails with a homemade dress running around their farm, chasing chickens, and laughing as she went. How I marveled at and loved this woman!

Grandma chuckled again. "We had a pig named Bill. He was as big as a refrigerator! I used to go out and watch him wallow around in the mud, making his snorting noises. He seemed to like having me out there with him. He would roll around and kick his feet in the air. I sure loved that pig!"

"I didn't know you had pigs growing up," I said.

"Yep. Over the years my pa had cows, pigs, chickens, a few goats, and of course lots of stray dogs and cats. We basically had our own farmland zoo!" She chuckled again.

"Sure sounds like simpler times," I said, not smiling now.

"Yes, in a way it was, Wyatt. But it was also hard times. We didn't have many clothes and rarely went to get groceries. We ate what we grew, raised, or shot. Some winters we didn't have a lot to eat, although they were good times through it all, though, because we had each other. I wouldn't trade all the money in the world for that, Wyatt!"

I sighed. "Yep, sure does sound like you had a lot of love in your family, Grandma. I wish our family growing up was more like yours."

Grandma studied me with a frown. "I know your growing up years weren't easy, Wyatt. I'm sorry your dad wasn't there for you more. I prayed a lot for you and the other kids."

I patted her hand. "I know, Grandma, and you were there for us as well. I always wanted to be at your house growing up. I have so many great memories of my times with you!"

Grandma's eyes filled with tears. "And those were great memories for me as well, Wyatt. I loved having you at my home and loved sitting next to you at church, even when you laughed at my singing!" She smiled.

I leaned over and hugged her, tears welling in my eyes too. Through my pain and struggle, this sweet woman was a constant in my life. She never wavered in her love and commitment to me. Consistency is such a key need for people in this broken world.

"What other stories do you remember growing up, Grandma?" I asked, leaning back in my chair.

"Well, let's see. I remember going to the county fair in

Cassville with family and friends. It was something we looked forward to every year! I can still smell the homemade apple cider, barbecue brisket, and fried pork rinds!"

"Did they have rides back then?"

Grandma laughed. "Of course they did, Wyatt! We also had cars too!"

I chuckled. "Okay, sorry."

"I liked riding all the rides, and they also had lots of animals you could feed or pet. When I was little that was my favorite. I've always loved animals, especially horses and goats."

She smiled. "Pa would always hold my hand when we walked around the fair, and he had this whistle when he walked. I don't even know if he realized he was whistling. It was like a bird singing in the morning. It always made me feel safe."

Grandma looked at me and winked, another tear escaping down her cheek.

I drove home after our visit, reflecting on my conversation with Grandma. Her stories got me thinking about my life. *What stories could I tell my grandkids someday about my childhood?* I grew somber thinking about this, realizing my childhood memories were often dark or bland. I'm sure there were pockets of pleasant memories. Still, most filtered through the tension and conflict between my parents and the poverty and bitterness after my dad left us.

I then thought about what memories my kids would hopefully have someday. I vowed to myself that their memories would be different from mine. Their lives would be full of color, not grey and fuzzy. My wife would be an awesome mother, and I would strive to be a better dad than my own.

I sighed. Suddenly I found myself talking to the God I wasn't sure existed.

"Lord, please heal my wife. Please give us a chance to be parents. Please help us to love our kids as Grandma Mabel's parents loved her. Please make yourself real to me so I can believe again and be a good example to my kids."

I drove on, marveling that I had just spoken with God again.

13

The Bible Piece

My life drifted on. I grew weary of my Walmart job. With the daily grind of hearing fellow employees complaining about mundane matters, customers griping about prices and not having in stock what they wanted, and higher managers nitpicking me on various issues, my willpower to get up each morning for work slowly ebbed.

I sighed, looking over at my wife, asleep on the couch. My fatigue from work quickly turned to worry as I studied her face, so drawn and pale. The chemo treatments attacked Mary's cancer but also drained her vitality and joy. My worry grew to anger once again as I thought about God amid this mixture of the mundane and heavy trials.

I called in sick to work the following day and decided to visit my grandma and Marcus. I especially wanted encouraging words from Marcus, who had become my unlikely friend. I had never had a black friend before. I had never considered myself as racist; however, hearing Marcus' story made me realize how ignorant I was of the racial divide in our country.

I waved to Marcus, sitting in his usual spot. Today I would see him first before spending time with Grandma.

"Well, isn't this a surprise!" Marcus said and laughed as I

approached. "I usually see you on the weekend, Wyatt. What's the occasion?"

"I decided to take the day off of work."

"You doing okay?" A look of concern crossed Marcus' face.

"I'm okay, just tired. I needed a break."

Marcus nodded. "I understand. Well, I'm glad you came to see me. I always enjoy our visits. I hope you do too."

I smiled. "I sure do, Marcus. I appreciate your wisdom and encouragement. I've enjoyed our talks."

"Good! I'm happy to hear you say so, Wyatt!"

I stared at Marcus. Here he sat in a wheelchair, far from family, with little independence, with such joy and enthusiasm every time I saw him. I envied his outlook and felt sudden shame for my own attitude at that moment.

Marcus interrupted my thoughts. "Are you ready to talk about the next piece of my puzzle, Wyatt?" He held a piece up, smiling.

"Sure. What's this piece called?

"Well, now, I call this here piece The Bible."

I frowned. The Bible had become a sore spot with me over the years. I stopped reading it regularly after my sister's death. It symbolized to me God's betrayal. I also struggled with its complexity, with the God of the Old Testament seemingly crueler and more vindictive than the God of the New Testament supposedly embodied in Jesus.

Marcus noticed my frown. "Do you have struggles with the Bible, Wyatt?"

"Honestly, yes," I answered, still frowning. "I have lots of questions on its reliability since it was written by men a long, long time ago."

"Fair point, Wyatt. Let's take a broad-based view of the

Bible first. I think over the years there have been lots of misunderstandings of the Bible. For one, it's referred to as a book. In reality it's a collection of sixty-six different writings of various styles, written over a period of fifteen hundred years on three continents by over forty different authors. Today the Bible has been translated into over seven hundred languages, and the New Testament in over an additional fifteen hundred languages!"

Marcus leaned forward. "And with all those different authors, and different genres of writing over all that time, a story emerges from the Bible. It's God's story. It's God's relationship with us human beings made in His image. It's a powerful story, bathed in history, of a God pursuing those He created."

"But how can you know it's true?" I persisted.

"Yes, good question. For me, I believe the Bible to be true for several reasons. The first, and for me the most important, is this—it has changed my life. Hebrews 4:12 says,

> *For the word of God is living and active, sharper than any two-edged sword, piercing to the division of soul and of spirit, of joints and of marrow, and discerning the thoughts and intentions of the heart.*

"I believe in God's Word, the Bible, because it has rung true in my life."

"Well, that's all good for you, Marcus, and I believe the Bible has brought you direction and comfort. But why doesn't it do that for so many others? It's from so long ago. How do we know God inspired it?"

Marcus smiled. "I enjoy these conversations, Wyatt! My heart was changed by the Bible but also my mind. Folks think you must check your brain at the door to believe in Christianity and the Bible. That's simply not true."

Marcus pulled out a piece of paper from his shirt pocket with a pen. He placed it on the table next to his puzzle and started writing.

"There are several other reasons why I believe the Bible is inspired by God and can be trusted, Wyatt. One, archeological evidence. Two, prophecies in the Bible fulfilled. Three, New Testament manuscriptal evidence. And four, the historical evidence for the resurrection. These four main areas of evidence convince my mind of the Bible being God-inspired and also have helped change my heart as well."

"Tell me about each reason, please." I was genuinely interested.

Marcus smiled. "Glad to! Let's start with the archeological evidence. The Bible is based on history, specifically history mainly in the Middle East. Many places mentioned in the Bible are not around today, so for years, skeptics mocked the Bible as fantasy or mythology, not history. But archeology over the years has turned up evidence that towns and communities mentioned in the Bible did exist! Findings also show the reliability and accuracy of biblical transcription over the years."

"Can you give examples?" I asked.

"Sure. The most important instance in my mind is the finding of the Dead Sea Scrolls back in 1947. Shepherds found the scrolls in caves on the western side of the Dead Sea. In those scrolls, almost every book of the Old Testament was found in fragments, dating back from the first to third century BC. In fact, a complete scroll of Isaiah was found! Scientists discovered that in comparing the writings of Scripture from these scrolls to biblical texts over a thousand years later, only minimal changes in a few wordings were found. No change in meaning whatsoever! The finding showed the accuracy and consistency of the Old Testament biblical text dating back over two thousand years ago."

Marcus spoke with enthusiasm. "In the ancient town of Tel Dan, Israel, several archeological finds have validated Scripture. In 1993, excavators at Tel Dan uncovered an inscription that translated as 'house of David,' dating back to the ninth century BC. Also, in Tel Dan today, we have an ancient Canaanite Gate dating back four thousand years. Abraham of the Old Testament likely walked through this gate!

"I could share many more archeological examples, such as many cities in the Old Testament that at one time skeptics said were mythical cities. Yet years later, remains and names mentioned in ancient writings were discovered, such as the seacoast city of Tyre."

"You mentioned prophecy?"

"Yes!" Marcus said. "Prophecy to me is a fascinating piece of my puzzle on why I believe! The Old Testament contains lots of prophecies fulfilled during the years before Christ, but what fascinates me the most is that from hundreds to thousands of years before Jesus was born, there were prophecies, or predictions, about Him, such as where He would be born and the manner of His death."

In my mind, when I think of prophecies, I think of Old Testament prophets predicting doom for the nation of Israel for their disobedience to God. It was all about God's fierce wrath and indignation.

Marcus continued. "For example, in Micah 5:2, some eight hundred years before Jesus was born, the prophet predicted the Messiah would be born in the town of Bethlehem. The prophet talked about what a small town it was, yet it would be the birthplace of the One who would save His people. In Isaiah 7:14, about seven hundred years before Jesus' birth, the prophet predicted, 'Therefore the Lord himself will give you a sign: The virgin will conceive and give birth to a son and will call him Immanuel.'"

Marcus looked at me and leaned close. He almost whispered. "Immanuel means 'God with us!' Isn't that amazing! Over seven centuries before Mary, a virgin gave birth to Jesus in Bethlehem, a prophet named Isaiah predicted it would happen, and eight centuries before, the prophet Micah predicted where it would happen.

"On top of that, scientific dating shows the Dead Sea scrolls I mentioned before were written hundreds of years before Jesus was born, and the prophecies of His life and death mapped out, especially in Isaiah 53, showcase a miracle of prediction on the grandest scale."

In my years of going to church, I hadn't read the Old Testament much. It seemed outdated and boring. I just thought it was history. I didn't read the prophets. This was new to me.

Marcus continued. "Isaiah predicts in a powerful way how and why this Messiah would die for you and me, Wyatt. In Isaiah 53:5 he says,

> *But he was pierced for our transgressions, he was crushed for our iniquities; the punishment that brought us peace was on him, and by his wounds we are healed.*

"In the New Testament, it shares He was pierced on the cross when they hammered spikes in His hands and feet, and when a soldier drove a spear through Him to ensure He was dead.

And Isaiah says, 'by his wounds we are healed.' Seven centuries before Jesus was born and lived thirty-three years and died on the cross, this prophet predicted it would all happen. Isn't that amazing, Wyatt?"

I nodded. "Yes, that's amazing, indeed. Are there other prophecies about Jesus in the Old Testament?"

Marcus smiled. "Oh yes, Wyatt. There are many more, both in the prophets, in the Psalms, and even way back in the beginning in Genesis!"

"Really?"

"Yes, indeed!" Marcus picked his Bible up from the table by his puzzle and began thumbing to the beginning of the Book.

"Yes, here it is. In Genesis 3:15, it says,

> *And I will put enmity between you and the woman, and between your offspring and hers; he will crush your head, and you will strike his heel.*

"God is talking here about the serpent, the devil. Eve's future offspring, Jesus, is shown here in His battle with the evil one. Jesus will die on the cross, but by His death and subsequent resurrection from the dead, the head of Satan and His plan of destruction will be crushed."

My heart stirred. All my life I felt I believed because my grandmother believed, and everyone I went to church with believed. I trusted them. But the weight of a broken world and my broken heart caused fissures of doubt to slowly grow and spread in my soul. I never really investigated faith. I just assumed it. And when my heart grew more bitter from life, I discarded it like an old blanket. Now, however, I was hearing evidence for faith from this kind man, an unlikely new friend who, to my shame, I would never have considered getting to know in the past because of the color of his skin. Now, that didn't seem to matter at all.

Marcus turned the pages of his Bible with his weathered hands. "Now for me, Wyatt, the verses in the Bible that most profoundly speak of the Messiah, Jesus, are found again in the whole chapter of Isaiah 53, again some six to seven hundred years before He was born. Let's see here."

With his wire-framed reading glasses on the lower edge of his nose, Marcus slowly turned the pages until he found his mark.

"Yes, sir, right here. Isaiah 53. I'm going to read the whole chapter if that's okay with you, Wyatt."

"Yes, go ahead," I said.

"Okay. Here goes . . .

Who has believed what he has heard from us? And to whom has the arm of the Lord been revealed? For he grew up before him like a young plant, and like a root out of dry ground; he had no form or majesty that we should look at him, and no beauty that we should desire him. He was despised and rejected by men, a man of sorrows and acquainted with grief; and as one from whom men hide their faces he was despised, and we esteemed him not. Surely, he has borne our griefs and carried our sorrows; yet we esteemed him stricken, smitten by God, and afflicted. But he was pierced for our transgressions; he was crushed for our iniquities; upon him was the chastisement that brought us peace, and with his wounds we are healed.

All we like sheep have gone astray; we have turned—everyone—to his own way; and the Lord has laid on him the iniquity of us all. He was oppressed, and he was afflicted, yet he opened not his mouth; like a lamb that is led to the slaughter, and like a sheep that before its shearers is silent, so he opened not his mouth. By oppression and judgment, he was taken away; and as for his generation, who considered that he was cut off out of the land of the living, stricken for the transgression of my people? And they made his grave with the wicked and with a rich man in his death, although he had done no violence, and there was no deceit in his mouth. Yet it was the will of the Lord to crush him; he has put him to grief; when his soul makes an offering for guilt, he shall see his offspring; he shall prolong his days; the will of the Lord shall prosper in his hand.

Out of the anguish of his soul he shall see and be satisfied; by his knowledge shall the righteous one, my servant, make many to be accounted righteous, and he shall bear the iniquities. Therefore, I will divide him a portion with the many, and he shall divide the spoil with the strong, because he poured out his soul to death and was numbered with the transgressors; yet he bore the sin of many and makes intercession for the transgressors.

Marcus stared at the print for a moment, shaking his head. "It always astounds me, Wyatt, how accurate this prophecy is toward Jesus. Hundreds of years before He entered this world, God spoke these words through Isaiah predicting the manner and reason of Jesus' death."

It struck me as well. The words seemed such an accurate description of the manner of Jesus' death and the reason for His death . . . for us. The sacrificial Lamb giving Himself for all of us strayed sheep.

Marcus held his Bible up in the air. "The next convincing evidence for me is the manuscriptal evidence for the New Testament. In all, there are over twenty-four thousand manuscripts in existence of the New Testament. That's far more than any other work of antiquity. To visualize this, a stack of manuscripts for the average classical writer from antiquity would measure about four feet high. Compare that to more than a mile if you stacked all the New Testament manuscripts and two and a half miles high for the entire Bible!"

"But aren't these manuscripts actually copies from the original writings?" I asked.

"Of course," Marcus said. "The original manuscripts of the New Testament and Old Testament, and all other works of antiquity, have long ago turned into dust. The difference is we see the copies over the centuries of the New Testament agree with each other. Their accuracy in detail is remarkable. Also, we have copies of the New Testament within a couple of generations from the writing of the originals. In contrast, in other ancient documents, you are looking at five to ten centuries of time between the original and the earliest surviving copy."

I persisted. "But how do we know the copies are accurate to the original writings? Wouldn't there be changes over all these years?"

Marcus smiled. "Good question, Wyatt." Historians admit there have been minor variations of wording, but never meaning. According to Norman Geisler, in addition to having far more surviving manuscripts than any other book of antiquity, the New Testament has also remained in a far purer form. Geisler estimates 99.5 percent pure!"

"Wow. That's impressive," I said.

"Yes, it is," Marcus said, still smiling.

I looked at Marcus. "You also mentioned the resurrection?"

"Ah, yes, the resurrection. The reality is, the resurrection is the crux of the Christian faith." He looked down and began thumbing through his Bible again.

"Here it is. First Corinthians 15:12-19 reads:

> *Now if Christ is proclaimed as raised from the dead, how can some of you say that there is no resurrection of the dead? But if there is no resurrection of the dead, then not even Christ has been raised. And if Christ has not been raised, then our preaching is in vain, and your faith is in vain. We are even found to be misrepresenting God, because we testified about God that he raised Christ, whom he did not raise if it is true that the dead are not raised. For if the dead are not raised, not even Christ has been raised. And if Christ has not been raised, your faith is futile, and you are still in your sins. Then those also who have fallen asleep in Christ have perished. If in Christ we have hope in this life only, we are of all people most to be pitied.*

Marcus looked at me with earnest eyes. "I want to talk with you about the resurrection in greater detail, Wyatt, because the resurrection is one of the main factors that separates Christianity from other religious beliefs. Mohammad is still in his grave. Buddha is still in his grave. According to the resurrection, however, Jesus is alive now and forevermore. If this is true, Christianity is true. If He did not rise from the grave, we are wasting our time following Him. It's that simple."

Marcus' words were blunt and stunning. I sat there staring at him. I knew of the resurrection from Easter services. Still, the event was so long ago and seemed like a fable, not history.

"Is there really evidence, historical evidence, for the resurrection?" I asked.

"Yes, Wyatt. There is, indeed," Marcus said. "But let's hold that for another day. I'm getting tired, and that will be a long conversation indeed."

I sat speechless, staring at my friend. While my soul was still deeply bruised, my mind was absorbing information I had never heard before concerning evidence for the Bible's validity and, with that, the truth of Christianity. This piece of the puzzle stirred both my mind and brought a touch of balm to my battered soul. I wanted to learn more.

14

COURTING MARY

After I visited with Grandma and Marcus, I drove home. The discussion about the Bible was revealing and encouraging. In all my years attending church, I never heard the evidence Wyatt mentioned. In fairness, much of the fault fell on me due to my lack of attention, especially as I entered my teen years. But part of the blame also rested on the shoulders of church leadership, who seemed to put more stock in filling the pews and the offering plate than true discipleship and growth of its members. I'm not saying that's how it is in every church, just in my experience.

I walked into a quiet house. Mary lay on the couch, asleep, with an open book across her chest. I sat next to her and stared at her peaceful face. My heart swelled as I studied her eyes, cheekbones, and pouty lips. She had such a tender, gentle face matching her gentle, kind spirit.

My thoughts rushed back to one of our early encounters. It was at a church picnic on Swan Creek. Mary's family owned a local grocery store and was well-known in the community. Mary was a grade behind me. I was a junior in high school at the time. I had known her from school but had never noticed her until watching her playing volleyball with others. Her hearty laugh turned my head as she tried to hit the ball over the net, only to see it go sideways into the nearby basketball court. I ran over, grabbed the ball, and brought it to her. She smiled and thanked me, and my heart rate quickened.

Grandma Mable noticed the exchange, and when I walked over to her, she smiled.

"That Mary Pickens is one nice girl, Wyatt," she said. "You need to ask her out."

I smiled at my recollection. Grandma was never one to hold back!

I remember watching Mary the next few days at school. Our eyes met in the hallways a few times, and we smiled. Each time that same swelling in my heart repeated, my nerves would take over, and my eyes quickly diverted.

Finally, I gathered the courage to walk up to Mary after school in the parking lot and ask her if she wanted to go see a movie the upcoming weekend with me. I still remember her shy smile, but she looked me in the eyes and said yes, but I would have to come to her house and meet her parents.

Her parents were not at all like my parents. They welcomed me into their home, though her dad did ask me many questions about myself and what we would do on our date, what time the movie would be over, and exactly what time he expected us back at the house. I respected his protective hand on his daughter and made sure always to have Mary back at home on or before the time he gave.

Our first date quickly became a second date the following weekend. From then on, we were a couple, walking together in the school hallway, holding hands, talking on the phone almost every night, and sitting by each other in church. I fell deeply in love with Mary, knowing even at our young age she would one day be my wife.

Though kind, Mary exhibits a stubborn streak too. If she disagrees with me on something, she will stand up to me with a ferocity that sometimes shocks me. Early in our marriage, that created tension, but as we worked out our differences and grew to understand each other on a deeper level, I began to see her stubbornness as a great strength, an endearing quality. I know now I can share my thoughts, ideas, and frustrations with her, and she will honestly share her opinions. Invariably, she helps me to rethink matters from a more comprehensive viewpoint.

I truly love her.

Mary stirred. Her eyes opened, and she smiled as she noticed me.

"Is it morning yet?" she asked as she yawned and stretched her arms straight up.

"Almost," I smiled. It's about five p.m. You were sleeping hard. How are you feeling?" I reached over and gently brushed the hair back from her face.

"I'm feeling pretty good, just tired. How was your visit with your grandma and Marcus?"

I leaned back on the couch. "Grandma slept for most of our visit. I spent a good amount of time with Marcus. He's one smart man!"

"What did you talk about?"

"He shared why we can trust the Bible as being the Word of God."

Mary sat up and looked at me. "Was that good for you?"

I sighed. "It gave me a lot to think about for sure. It frustrates me that I grew up in the church and didn't know or learn the things Marcus shared with me today."

Mary reached over and grabbed my hand. "I'm really glad you met Marcus. He's been good for you. I'd like to meet him myself soon."

I nodded. "I would like that too. I think you would really like him."

"I'm sure I would. It seems to me God has put him in our life at just the right time."

I stared at Mary. Her eyes began to glisten with emotion. Between her battle with cancer, our struggle to have children, and my own spiritual battles, I knew that her faith had not wavered through it all. I also knew she had been praying for me daily.

Mary's faith was a quiet but consistent commitment. Before bed nightly, she would read her Bible and journal. In the mornings, no matter how bad she felt from the chemo, I would see her in her living room chair with the lamp on, reading and praying. While my faith drifted, her faith remained solid and anchored.

She was my anchor.

I reached over and hugged Mary. "I sure love you," I said, holding her tightly.

"I love you too, honey," she said, her voice cracking. "I just want you to know deep in your heart God loves you too."

"I'm working on it."

After supper, Mary and I sat on the couch together and watched TV. I held Mary close as she drifted off again to sleep. After I woke her to go to bed, I decided to sit on our front porch and enjoy the warm night sky. As I stared at the stars and full moon, I thought again about my conversation with Marcus. Perhaps I needed to begin rereading my dust-covered Bible and see if God would freshly reveal Himself.

I rose up from my chair and went back into the house. My Bible lay on our bookshelf. I picked it up and stared at it. I opened it to the page that showed my name and the date I received the Bible. Grandma Mabel gave me the Bible back when I was twelve years old. I smiled, remembering Grandma instructing me to read John because "John really knew Jesus well."

I sat back on the couch, opened my Bible, and began reading the book of John. "Lord," I prayed. "Please show me Yourself."

15

Jesus: The Incarnation

It had been a couple of weeks since my last visit to Grandma and Marcus. Mary and I got away the weekend before to Eureka Springs, Arkansas. We enjoyed a much-needed time away from our regular lives to focus on each other. Mary felt better after her chemo treatments. Just two more treatments remained.

Grandma was sitting in her recliner in her room when I walked in. I always preferred seeing her sitting up as opposed to lying in bed.

"Hi Grandma!" I said as I walked into the room.

"Well, there's my boy!" she answered, smiling. "I've missed you!"

"I've missed you too. Sorry I didn't visit last weekend. Mary and I went to Eureka Springs."

"Oh, I love that place," Grandma said, still smiling. "Your grandfather and I used to go to the Passion Play every summer there. Some nice places to eat there as well."

I moved close to her as I scooted a chair up. "How have you been feeling?"

"I've been feeling pretty well," she said. "My appetite has been good this past week."

"Good. Your eyes look brighter."

"The better to see you with, my dear." She chuckled. It was good to see Grandma happy.

"How is sweet Mary?" she asked, placing her hand on mine.

"She's doing better. Almost done with her chemo treatments."

"Praise God! I've been praying for her, Wyatt."

"Thanks, Grandma. That means a lot to us both."

Grandma studied me. "And how are you doing, Wyatt? How is your heart through all of this?"

I paused. *How is my heart? I just don't know.*

"It's good," I simply said, not wanting to explore the topic further. "Tell me another story about your younger years, Grandma."

I could tell from Grandma's face that she knew I was changing the subject.

"Did I tell you about the time I snuck out of my house one night?"

"What? Why did you do that?"

"Well, because Norma Jean down the road tapped on my window and said let's go to town. She had eased her car into our driveway and wanted to go look for boys in Branson!"

I laughed. "Well, did you find any?"

"Oh sure!" Grandma smiled. "We just didn't know what to do with them when we found them! So, we drove back over to Swan Creek and swam and talked until very late."

"Did you get caught?"

"Nope. My ma and pa were both heavy sleepers. I might have slipped out a few more times when I was young!" She winked at me.

After visiting Grandma for about another half hour, I could tell her eyes were getting heavy, so I put a blanket over her and helped her recline her chair back. As she closed her eyes, I kissed her forehead and told her I loved her. She smiled. "Sure love you too, Wyatt."

I took my usual seat beside Marcus as he struggled with his puzzle.

"Wyatt, they sure make puzzles a lot more difficult these days!" He shook his head.

"Don't give up, Marcus!" I smiled as I studied his slowly converging picture.

He looked at me and chuckled. "Never!"

I observed Marcus' face. His dark skin was weathered and leathery from years of living. His hair was white as snow, closely cropped on his head. His scraggly white beard and recently grown mustache matched his hair. His eyes were still bright and eager, kind yet searching.

Marcus interrupted my thoughts.

"I have a new piece of my puzzle to discuss with you, son. Are you ready for it?"

"Sure," I said. Let's hear it!"

Marcus slowly raised a center piece from inside his border wall of pieces. "I call this piece the Incarnation of Jesus."

"I remember the word Incarnation, Marcus, but can't remember exactly what it means. Can you refresh me?" I asked.

"Sure!" Marcus answered with enthusiasm. "Let me read you what it means from John chapter one."

Marcus lifted his glasses from his front pocket, slid them on, and then pulled out his worn brown Bible from the edge of his table and slowly leafed through it.

"Ah, here we go. John chapter one starts out with this:

In the beginning was the Word, and the Word was with God, and the Word was God. He was in the beginning with God. All things came into being through Him, and without Him not one thing came into being. What has come into being in Him was life, and the life was the light of all people. The light shines in the darkness, and the darkness did not overcome it.

Marcus looked up at me.

"The Word here is Jesus, Wyatt. It says here Jesus was in the beginning with God, and He is God."

Marcus looked back down at his Bible.

"Let's skip over to verse fourteen. Here's what it says…

And the Word became flesh and lived among us, and we have seen His glory, the glory as of a father's only son, full of grace and truth.

Marcus looked back up, his eyes earnest and passionate.

"The incarnation is this, Wyatt. God the Son entering our world, full of grace and truth. This piece of the puzzle is one of the central pieces of why I believe, Wyatt. It's so fantastic and unbelievable, but so amazing and revealing of the character of God."

"But how do you know Jesus really lived?" I asked. This question of the historical validity of Jesus had been bothering me for some time.

Marcus reached for his coffee and took a sip. He looked at me and smiled. "Good question, Wyatt. I will tell you at the outset that almost all historians, whether believers or not, admit that the evidence that Jesus lived is undisputed. Let's see why this is the case."

Marcus folded his hands on the table and leaned forward. "First of all, the four Gospels, Matthew, Mark, Luke, and John, give excellent eyewitness evidence for the life of Jesus. They were written by either the disciples themselves, Matthew and John, or close associates of the disciples and Paul, the primary writer of much of the New Testament. Mark was a close associate of Peter, and Luke, the physician, traveled extensively with Paul."

"These accounts were written by Jesus' followers. How do we know they didn't make up some of the more extraordinary events of Jesus' life to feed into their new religion?" I asked.

Marcus smiled. "Yes, I've heard this question many times from students, Wyatt. When you read over the Gospels, if the disciples wanted to make things up, don't you think they would have painted themselves in more flattering colors?" He laughed.

"What do you mean?"

"Peter, for example," Marcus answered. "One minute Jesus is telling him he's going to be the rock of the church. The next minute after Peter corrects Jesus when He says He's going to be crucified, Jesus calls him Satan! And the time Peter sinks in the water while the other disciples are cowered in the boat. There are many other examples where the disciples are not seen in a complimentary light. If they were making this story up, you would think they would have made themselves look better."

"I can see that," I said.

"More importantly," Marcus continued. "If this story was a lie, why would the disciples allow themselves to be killed or in John's case, exiled to the Island of Patmos for not renouncing the story of Jesus and His resurrection? If the Gospel accounts were made up and the heat was put on them, don't you think they would have recanted to save their own skins?"

"You would think so," I said.

Marcus shifted in his seat and pointed back at the middle piece he had been holding.

"Historically, Jesus is not just mentioned in the Gospels. Other writers who were not followers of Jesus refer to Him in their writings. This is the main reason even unbelieving historians say Jesus of Nazareth was a real person who walked the earth."

This intrigued me. I had never had this conversation about the historical Jesus outside the Bible records. I leaned closer to Marcus.

"For example," Marcus continued. "Josephus was a first century Jewish historian. He was not a follower of Jesus but mentioned him in his writings."

Marcus seemed prepared. I noticed he had a book called *The Case for Christ* by Lee Strobel. He thumbed through it silently. Suddenly he stopped and smiled.

"Here it is!" he said. "This is a quote from one of Josephus' writings." Marcus read out loud:

> *About this time there lived Jesus, a wise man, if indeed one ought to call him a man. For he was one who wrought surprising feats and was a teacher of such people as accept the truth gladly. He won over many Jews and many of the Greeks. He was the Christ. When Pilate, upon hearing him accused by men of the highest standing among us, had condemned him to be crucified, those who had in the first place come to love him did not give up their affection for him. On the third day he appeared to them restored to life for the prophets of God had prophesied these and countless other marvelous things about him. And the tribe of Christians, so called after him, has still to this day not disappeared.*

Marcus looked up after reading. "Again, Josephus was not a follower of Jesus, but he shares in his book on the history of Jewish thought about Him here. Most historians today believe this quote to be authentic, though there are opinions of some interpolations."

"What are interpolations?"

"Interpolations are basically a few phrases possibly added by Christian copyists, such as the phrase above 'if indeed one ought to call him a man' and the statement 'He was the Christ.' Nevertheless, in Josephus' writings he talks about Jesus, and the brother of Jesus, James, talking about him being delivered over to be stoned for following Jesus. Historians see Josephus as a highly credible historian. His accounts of the Jewish War in the first century have proven to be very accurate. They have been corroborated from archaeological excavations at a place called Masada. Because of that, and Josephus' non-allegiance to Jesus, the fact that he mentions Jesus in his writings carries a lot of weight."

"Okay," I said. "That's pretty compelling. Are there any other examples?"

"Yes, indeed, there are. In 115 AD, a Roman historian, Tacitus, stated that Nero persecuted the Christians as scapegoats to divert suspicion away from himself for the fire that destroyed Rome in 64 AD."

Marcus turned the page in *The Case for Christ* book.

"This is from Tacitus:

> Nero fastened the guilt and inflicted the most exquisite tortures on a class hated for the abominations, called Christians by the populace. Christus, from whom the name had its origin, suffered the extreme penalty during the reign of Tiberius at the hands of one of our procurators, Pontius

> Pilatus, and a most mischievous superstition, thus checked for the moment, again broken out not only in Judaea, the first source of the evil, but even in Rome.

Marcus looked up from his reading. "Tacitus was no follower of Jesus but wrote about Him here as the One who started the Christian movement. Scholars readily believe the superstition referred to in this writing is the disciples' claim of Jesus' resurrection.

"Another Roman, Pliny the Younger, referred to Christianity in his writings. He arrested many Christians for not recanting their belief in their risen Savior. Let's see. Here it is. Strobel says in his book that Pliny talks about the Christians he arrested in one of his letters to Emperor Trajan:

> I have asked them if they are Christians, and if they admit it, I repeat the question a second and third time, with a warning of the punishment awaiting them. If they persist, I order them to be led away for execution; for, whatever the nature of their admission, I am convinced that their stubbornness and unshakable obstinacy ought not to go unpunished . . . they had met regularly before dawn on a fixed day to chant verses alternately amongst themselves in honor of Christ as if to a god, and also to bind themselves by oath, not for any criminal purpose, but to abstain from theft, robbery, and adultery.

Marcus looked up. "This writing is believed to be written around 111 AD and shows the rapid spread of Christianity at that time. It shows Jesus was worshiped as God and that many of His followers were willing to suffer and die for their belief in Him. All this was written by one who was against the spread of this new religion.

This was fascinating to me. I didn't realize there was evidence like this outside the Bible that Jesus lived on earth. He was a real person!

Marcus coughed. "Excuse me, got a little cold. So, you can see the evidence confirms Jesus did exist. The bigger question is this: What was He like, and is He really who He said He was?"

I nodded. If Jesus did live, understanding His character and, on a deeper level, who He was and why He was born would be valuable.

Marcus coughed again and took another sip of his coffee. "Wyatt, when I began reading the Gospels while asking in my heart and mind what Jesus was like, my understanding and appreciation for His character grew tremendously!"

"How so?" I asked.

"I can explain it the best I can, Wyatt, but honestly, I invite you to do the same for yourself. Ask God to reveal His character in Jesus as you read in Matthew, Mark, Luke, and John. Ask Him to show you what He truly is like."

I sighed. The Bible had been gathering dust in my bedroom over the past year. "I did recently start reading in John." I looked at Marcus, uncommitted to his challenge.

Marcus noticed my hesitation. "Keep going, Wyatt. Finish reading John and then read the other Gospels."

Marcus quickly picked up his piece again. "The heart of this piece of the incarnation of Jesus is that He Himself claimed to be equal with God. This is the basis of the doctrine of the Trinity—one God in three persons: the Father, the Son, and the Holy Spirit. Jesus was no mere man. He was God come to earth as man. Fully God, fully man. Those who try to say that yes, Jesus really lived but was merely a great teacher or even a great prophet of God miss the mark. Jesus did not give them the option."

Marcus turned to the inside cover of his Bible. "I have a quote from C.S. Lewis, who expresses this far better than I could. Here it is. Lewis says:

> I am trying here to prevent anyone saying the really foolish thing that people often say about Him [that is, Christ]: "I'm ready to accept Jesus as a great moral teacher, but I don't accept His claim to be God." That is the one thing we must not say. A man who was merely a man and said the sort of things Jesus said would not be a great moral teacher. He would either be a lunatic—on a level with the man who says he is a poached egg—or else he would be the Devil of Hell. You must make your choice. Either this man was, and is, the Son of God: or else a madman or something worse . . . You can shut Him up for a fool, you can spit at Him and kill Him as a demon; or you can fall at His feet and call Him Lord and God. But let us not come up with any patronizing nonsense about His being a great human teacher. He has not left that open to us. He did not intend to.

Marcus closed the book and looked silently at me. Then he slowly lifted the piece of the puzzle up toward me. "The incarnation of Jesus, along with his crucifixion and resurrection, are the greatest events in human history, Wyatt. In that moment in time, God of eternity intersected with humanity in space and time and walked among us in the form of Jesus of Nazareth. He walked on the pages of history for thirty-three years, and in that time started a movement that has forever changed the world.

"Our calendar is based on this life. Many of our holidays are based on this life. And by His words about Himself we are placed in a singular decision—accept him as the Son of God and Savior of the world or reject him as such. There is no middle ground."

I was taken aback by the force of Marcus' words. I sat back in my chair, staring at this wise man and now dear friend, shaken to the core. This piece of the puzzle seemed central and vital in understanding reality and truth. The picture was slowly getting clearer.

16

Grandma's Last Visit

The phone rang as I was dressing for work.

"Hello," I said, trying not to yawn.

"Hello, Wyatt," the voice on the phone said somberly. "This is Emily from Spring Hills Nursing Home. Your grandmother had a stroke in the night and has been rushed to the hospital in Branson. I wanted you to know. I'm so sorry."

My eyes welled up with tears. "Thanks for letting me know," I managed to say before hanging up.

I called into work to let them know about my grandma, then hugged my wife before heading to the hospital. Dark sadness enveloped me as I drove. Memories flooded in of special times with Grandma. Her encouraging smile, frequent hugs, and consistent input into my life shaped me into who I am today. She cared when my parents didn't seem to care.

I remember her going on walks with me when I was young. We would walk along Swan Creek looking for arrowheads, watch the fish splash in the water, and catch crawdads under rocks in neighboring Bull Creek. She constantly taught me things about nature and life. She always wove God into her lessons, how all the beauty of creation came from Him.

When tensions built at home, Grandma would always invite my siblings and me over to stay with her. Grandpa, like my dad, rarely interacted with us, but he still was kind. Grandpa would give me a quarter just about every time I came to visit. He didn't attend church with Grandma, but I noticed he always watched Billy Graham's Crusades on TV.

Grandma would make us excellent pies and peanut butter cookies. I enjoyed watching her bake, crisscrossing her cookies with a fork. She never hurried. Grandma hummed as she cooked, allowing me to help her mix the batter and later lick the bowl.

I pulled into the hospital parking lot, full of memories and emotions.

Grandma lay silently with her eyes closed. A nurse was checking her vitals as I stepped close to hold Grandma's hand.

"Are you her grandson, Wyatt?" the nurse asked.

"Yes."

"She was asking about you when she was awake."

"So she can speak?"

"Yes, but she doesn't stay awake long. She's very weak."

The nurse stepped out of the room, and I sat beside Grandma, holding her hand. I observed her white hair and wrinkled skin, remembering when her hair was darker and her skin smoother. A tear escaped my eye. Grandma showed more love and devotion to me than either of my parents. This hurt me to think this, but it was true. She had been my constant cheerleader, encourager, and advocate.

Her eyes slowly opened, and her head turned toward me.

"Wyatt, is that you?"

"Yes, Grandma. It's me. How are you?"

A small smile edged its way across her face. "I'm about to finish my race, I believe."

More tears flowed.

"I'm here with you, Grandma. I'll be here with you when you finish."

Grandma looked at me. The love in those worn eyes shone brightly. "I'm glad you're here, Wyatt. I sure love you."

"I love you too, Grandma." I buried my head on her bed next to her leg.

She reached out and slowly stroked my hair.

"Don't be sad, Wyatt. I know where I'm going. I'm ready for the next chapter! I'm ready to see loved ones I haven't seen in many years. Don't worry about me."

Her hand rested gently on my head. I lay there, remembering the many times, as a young boy, lying with my head in her lap on the couch while she rubbed my head and talked with me. Her steady presence in my life was an anchor and refuge for a boy with an uncertain and inconsistent homelife. I heard her gently humming an old hymn I knew she loved, "When the Roll Is Called Up Yonder." Her humming was shaky but sure and confident. Her faith, as it always had been, was carrying her now.

Her humming stopped, and her hand stopped moving.

I looked up and knew she was gone.

The machine started beeping, and a couple of nurses entered the room. Grandma had signed a do-not-resuscitate order months before in the nursing home, so they quietly turned off the machines. One of the nurses gently told me she was sorry. They walked out to give me more time.

I moved my chair closer to Grandma's face.

"You were always there for me, Grandma," I said, tears streaming down my face. "You loved me when my parents chose not to. You believed in me and always encouraged me. I will sure miss you."

I rose from my chair and kissed her forehead. Her face looked peaceful. Thoughts of where she was now, according to her confident faith, gave me hope, though my faith was still fragile and uncertain. I decided to talk with God.

"God, I know I have not been close to You and still struggle with believing You are real, but my sweet grandma believed in You. Please honor her now and give her a great reunion. She deserves it. Help me to truly believe in You again."

I stared at Grandma for a time, soaking in this goodbye moment. I knew I had phone calls to make to my wife and other family members that Grandma was gone. I dreaded some of those conversations.

Grandma's funeral was held at her old church, with family and longtime neighbors and friends attending. Grandma was buried in the old cemetery not far from her home. She rested with relatives from long ago near an ancient sycamore tree. Mary held my hand as she and I alone remained by Grandma's fresh gravesite.

I didn't visit Marcus that next weekend. I didn't want to go to the nursing home and not see Grandma there. I also didn't want to talk about God. In my heart, I knew I did believe in Him, and Marcus had helped me rediscover that. I think I was just mad at God for taking my grandma away, though deep in my heart, I knew she was ready.

I just missed her so much already. Her death caused the pieces of my puzzle to fall to the ground all over again, though in my heart, I knew how many of the pieces would eventually fit back together.

17

THE RESURRECTION PIECE 1

I decided not to see Marcus for another weekend. I grieved over my grandmother and couldn't bring myself to visit where she lived. I went through the motions at work, took care of Mary, and spent several evenings drinking a few beers and reflecting on my memories of Grandma.

Finally, the following Saturday morning, I lay in bed. Mary turned over.

"Honey, you need to go see Marcus."

"Why?" I said, yawning.

"Because I think you need to process this with him. I've also been thinking of him. He's probably grieving the loss of your grandma too."

I didn't even think about how this might be affecting Marcus. "Okay, I'll go," I said, though my body wanted to stay in bed.

I walked into the nursing home with a heavy heart and saw Marcus in his usual spot. When he saw me walking toward him, his face was not smiling.

"I wondered if you would ever come back, Wyatt," he said. Tears were welling up in his eyes.

Guilt swept over me like a thick cloud.

"I'm so sorry, Marcus. It's just been hard to come back here with Grandma gone."

Marcus nodded. "I understand, son, and wouldn't have blamed you if you never came back. I would have just missed seeing you, that's all."

I put my arm around him, and we hugged. I felt his hands shaking on my back.

I sat down next to him. His puzzle lay there. It looked like he hadn't made much progress since the last time I saw him.

"How are you doing, Wyatt?" Marcus asked.

I sighed. "I've been okay. There's a large hole in my heart now with Grandma gone. She was such a big part of my life growing up."

Marcus nodded. "Yes, I will miss our late-night chats in her room."

"Did you have many of those chats?"

Marcus chuckled. "Oh yes! I'd roll by just to wave to her, and she'd motion for me to come in. We'd laugh a lot, recalling our earlier years. Other times we'd both cry, sharing our heartaches and pains over the years as well."

Marcus shook his head. I noticed a stream of tears running down his cheek.

"I truly loved your grandma, Wyatt," Marcus said. "She always encouraged me and saw me as a person. I never felt she cared about the color of my skin. That's really rare."

I sat there in silence, ashamed I could not say the same. Marcus was the first black friend I ever made. Granted, there were not any black families in the area where I grew up, but from work and my travels, I had to admit I avoided meeting, let alone getting to know, folks who were different from me, whether that meant black, Latino, or any other culture other than my white, southern Missouri heritage. Anything else was unknown and uncomfortable.

In getting to know Marcus, I saw I had missed so much. I realized I needed to learn to be comfortable with being uncomfortable.

Marcus patted my hand. "I'm glad you're here, my boy. I've really missed you, indeed!"

"I missed you too, Marcus." I meant it.

We chatted about how he had been doing at the nursing home without Grandma. Marcus admitted not visiting with too many other residents. He mainly kept to himself and his puzzle, which he said he just stared at most of the time.

"Speaking of this blasted puzzle," Marcus said with a smile, "would you like to talk about another piece of why I believe?"

"Sure," I replied. "I really would."

Marcus picked up a piece with lots of colors in it. "This piece is a very important one of why I believe in Christianity as truth. I call it the resurrection."

Marcus looked at the piece in his hand as he continued.

"The resurrection, if true, is the greatest moment in the history of this world since creation, right alongside the incarnation and the cross. It is the culmination of Jesus' mission to save you and me, and all of humanity."

I whistled. "Wow, that's a big statement, Marcus."

"It certainly is, Wyatt. Paul himself in the Bible says as much. Let's see. Let me read it to you."

Marcus picked up his worn Bible and started thumbing through it, humming as he did so.

"Ah, here we go. First Corinthians 15:12-17. Here's what it says, Wyatt:

> *Now if Christ is proclaimed as raised from the dead, how can some of you say that there is no resurrection of the dead? But if there is no resurrection of the dead, then not even Christ has been*

> *raised. And if Christ has not been raised, then our preaching is in vain, and your faith is in vain. We are even found to be misrepresenting God, because we testified about God that he raised Christ, whom he did not raise if it is true that the dead are not raised. For if the dead are not raised, not even Christ has been raised. And if Christ has not been raised, your faith is futile, and you are still in your sins.*

Marcus looked at me as he held the Bible in his hands. "You see, Wyatt, the truth of Christianity rises or falls on the truth and reality of the resurrection. And the resurrection is not a myth but an historical event. As an historical event, we can investigate whether its historicity is valid and solid or weak and suspect."

I nodded. "I know many do not believe in Christianity because of the miracles, especially the resurrection. To them it is a fantasy belief because they have never seen a miracle."

Marcus looked at me. "What do you say?"

I hesitated. "I'm not sure. I want to believe in the resurrection because without it, life seems futile and hopeless. I want to believe Grandma has been resurrected. But it's hard to believe when I haven't seen miracles in my own life—only disappointment."

Marcus nodded. "Yes, when life is hard it's difficult to see outside our own pain. God understands, Wyatt. Let's take some time to look at the resurrection and what happened leading up to it and what happened afterwards. Maybe the evidence will shine light on the event."

Marcus pondered for a moment, seemingly in deep thought. He stroked his beard, looking upward. He then turned to me.

"Before we can discuss the resurrection, Wyatt, let's look

at the events that led up to this amazing event. Jesus was arrested by the religious leaders from trumped-up charges. The reality is they were threatened by Him and afraid He would take away their power and prestige with the people. Jealously and pride drove them."

Marcus leaned back in his chair and looked up. I could tell he was thinking hard.

"Through the late night they interrogated Him, beat Him, and spoke false accusations against Him. Early the next morning, they brought Him before Pontius Pilate. Pilate was the Roman prefect or governor under Emperor Tiberius. He saw no guilt in Jesus after interviewing Him, but because of the pressure of the religious leaders and the crowds, he turned Him over to be scourged and crucified."

"Scourged means He was whipped, right?" I asked.

Marcus nodded slowly. His eyes looked worn and sad. "Yes, Wyatt, but much worse. The Roman scourge, an historical weapon of bodily destruction, was often called a cat-o'-nine-tails. It was composed of several strands of leather tied to a handle. Pieces of metal and glass tied into each strand formed a terrifying and brutal agent against the flesh. If you have watched the movie *The Passion of the Christ*, you remember how bloody and torturous the Roman scourging is. Jesus went through this before His crucifixion."

Marcus continued. "At the Roman crucifixion, which was their usual method of public execution for the worst criminals and designed for physical and emotional torture, Jesus would have been laid on a vertical beam, with His arms stretched out on a connected horizontal beam, forming a cross. His hands would be staked at the base of the hand between the two bones of the wrist, and a single stake would be nailed through his feet crossed one over the other. Then they would drop the cross in a hole dug to hold it in place.

"Just think about this, Wyatt. Jesus had just had basically most if not all the skin shredded off his back. His face had been beaten. A crown of thorns had been jammed on His head. And in this horrible condition, He is nailed to this cross and left to be publicly humiliated in front of His mother, friends, and enemies alike."

I shook my head. "I can't imagine His suffering."

Marcus sighed. "Yes. And according to Scripture, He hung on the cross for six long hours. What amazes me, Wyatt, is the three instances toward the end of those six hours where Jesus showed compassion and love for others while suffering. The first was asking the Father to forgive those who were down below Him gambling for His clothes, the very ones who nailed Him to the cross. Then He looks at His earthly mother, Mary, and tells the disciple John to take her as his mother.

Finally, after one of the two thieves on crosses next to Jesus asks Jesus to remember Him, He looks at him and says the man will join Him in paradise. Amazing love on display even after being betrayed, forsaken, lied about, spit on, beaten, and mocked."

I looked down. I hadn't thought about what Jesus went through on the cross for years, probably not since watching the movie *The Passion of the Christ* with my wife.

Marcus' eyes glistened. "In the end, he said, 'It is finished,' and died. The Bible goes on to say that they begin breaking the legs of those on the cross, which was a way to speed up death before the beginning of the Passover. When they come to Jesus, they find He's already dead."

Marcus reached for his Bible and turned the pages. "Here

it is. Numbers 9:12 says, 'They shall leave none of it until the morning, nor break any of its bones; according to all the statute for the Passover they shall keep it.'"

Marcus looked at me. "These words spoken by Moses many centuries before Jesus came was another prophesy about the Messiah, the Lamb of God, fulfilled in Jesus. The legs of Jesus were not broken because He was already dead. However, to ensure He was indeed dead, a soldier took a spear and stuck it in Jesus' side. The Gospel of John said that water mixed with blood came out. Medical specialists state this means that the pericardial sac around Jesus' heart was punctured, clear evidence He was dead."

"How is that clear evidence?" I asked.

"Medical specialists have said that the water gushing out mixed with blood happens because of heart failure, resulting in the collection of fluid in the membrane around the heart, as well as around the lungs. It is likely that the spear in the side punctured the fluid in both places. Even if He wasn't dead before, a spear in His side after experiencing the Roman scourge and six hours of crucifixion would have certainly killed Him."

"Okay, that makes sense. I could not imagine lasting six hours hung by my hands and feet after being beaten. I remember, Marcus, hearing that the crucifixion torture was designed to cause the victim to slowly suffocate. Is that true?"

"Yes, I've read about that too, Wyatt. The weight of the body pulls down from the outstretched arms, putting pressure on the diaphragm. To get breath, the person would have to push up off their nailed feet, which of course would be very painful. Slowly the human yo-yo repetition to breathe causes the victim to become exhausted, unable to push up, then slowly suffocates."

I shook my head. "Such a horrible way to die."

"Indeed." Marcus nodded. "And think of this, Jesus said at any point, He could have called down twelve legions of angels—that's over seventy thousand angels! Yet He chose to endure the pain to pay the penalty for our sins. It was His love for us that sent Him to the cross, but it was His committed love for us that kept Him on the cross."

This last statement from Marcus touched a deep place in my heart. All my life, Christianity was a duty, a place to go on Sunday mornings. A set of rules to keep me from going wild. In my experience, I only saw the embodiment of Christ in my grandmother. I experienced only short snippets of that love from my parents. My slow drifting away from the person of Christ occurred through my own brokenness blended with a broken world. Hearing Marcus share Christ's deep commitment of love to me and all humanity stirred a deep longing in my heart, one I had squelched for many years.

Marcus looked at me in silence for a time, then spoke.

"After Jesus died, the soldiers took His body down. The Bible says Joseph of Arimathea, a rich man and council member who was also a secret disciple of Jesus, with Nicodemus, a Pharisee, treated the body with about seventy-five pounds of myrrh and aloes and wrapped the body in linen. They laid the body of Jesus in Joseph of Arimathea's tomb."

Marcus looked straight ahead as he spoke. "Jesus was gone."

18

THE RESURRECTION PIECE 2

I stared at Marcus. Tears were in his eyes. His lips trembled as he began to speak again.

"Jesus was gone, Wyatt. He died and was buried, but the greatest event in human history since His birth happened three days later. Jesus rose from the grave!"

Marcus wiped his tears away and smiled.

"The resurrection of Jesus shines the light on the truth of what He had been saying all along. He predicted His death, but He also predicted His resurrection."

I interrupted. "But Marcus, how can we know this really happened? It was over two thousand years ago. It seems like a fable to many."

Marcus nodded. "Yes, I know. Many don't believe in miracles because they have never seen one. Remember, the resurrection happened not in a fantasy storybook but in human history, so we need to look at human history to see if what happened seems plausible."

Marcus reached for his Bible sitting on the table by his puzzle. He leafed through the pages and stopped when he found his place.

"Here in Luke chapter 24, it talks about the resurrection. It says this:

> *But on the first day of the week, at early dawn, they came to the tomb, taking the spices that they had prepared. They found the stone rolled away from the tomb, but when they went in, they did not find the body. While they were perplexed about this, suddenly two men in dazzling clothes stood beside them. The women were terrified and bowed their faces to the ground, but the men said to them, "Why do you look for the living among the dead? He is not here but has risen. Remember how he told you, while he was still in Galilee, that the Son of Man must be handed over to sinners, and be crucified, and on the third day rise again." Then they remembered his words, and returning from the tomb, they told all this to the eleven and to all the rest.*

Marcus closed the Bible and set it gently back on his table.

"Here we see, Wyatt, the amazing event predicted by Jesus many times to His disciples. He had risen from the grave. The Gospels share many instances where Jesus appeared to the eleven, to Mary Magdalene, to seven disciples while they are fishing, to His earthly brother James, to Paul, and at one point to over five hundred people. These appearances happened over a period of forty days until His ascension mentioned in Acts chapter one."

"So other than these alleged appearances of Jesus, what evidence is there that the resurrection actually took place in history?" I asked.

Marcus leaned forward, smiling.

"You got some extra time today?"

"Sure," I said.

"Ok, then, let's get to it!" Marcus smiled. "First of all, there's a really good book on the resurrection called *The Case for the Resurrection of Jesus* by Gary Habermas and Michael Licona. I recommend it. In the book they talk about using what they call the minimal fact approach in giving evidence for the resurrection of Jesus. This means they only share evidence that is agreed upon by almost all historians because the data is so strong. They mention five facts that historians all agreed happened. First, Jesus in fact did die by crucifixion. Second, the disciples believed that Jesus appeared to them after His resurrection. Third, the persecutor of the early church, Paul, was suddenly changed and became a follower of Christ, writing most of the New Testament letters. Fourth, the skeptic James, brother of Jesus, was suddenly changed. And fifth, the tomb where Jesus' body was laid was empty."

Marcus paused, waiting to see if I had any questions. I remained silent, so he continued.

"Historians agree that the historical event of the crucifixion happened. Evidence comes not only from the Bible, where it is found in all four Gospels, but also other sources, including non-Christian sources, such as Josephus, a Jewish historian, Roman writers, and Greek writers."

"Are these writers from close to the time Jesus was crucified or centuries afterward?" I asked.

"These sources were from the same time period of the crucifixion, first and second century," said Marcus.

"Now, let's look at the second piece of evidence, that the disciples of Jesus believed that He rose and appeared to them. Evidence proves that Paul and James claimed He had risen and after this claim, their lives and actions were radically changed. They went from hiding to publicly proclaiming Jesus had risen. According to Habermas and Licona, the evidence for the disciples' claim and belief Jesus rose from the grave comes from three categories of sources. One, the testimony of Paul concerning the disciples' claims. Two, the oral tradition that was passed through the early church. And three, the written works of the early church."

Marcus continued. "Paul in his many letters in the New Testament talks about his close relationship with the disciples and discusses their belief that Jesus rose from the dead. As far as oral tradition, creeds were a popular way of passing along information that made it easy to memorize. One of the popular creeds is found in one of Paul's letters. First Corinthians 15, I believe."

Marcus reached for his Bible again and quickly found the verse he was looking for. "Ah, yes, First Corinthians 15:3-5. This is considered one of the most ancient creeds passed along orally after the death and resurrection of Jesus. It says,

> *For I delivered to you as of first importance what I also received, that Christ died for our sins according to the Scriptures, and that He was buried, and that He was raised on the third day according to the Scriptures, and that He appeared to Cephas, then to the twelve.*

Marcus closed the Bible and gently placed it back on the table.

"All four Gospels and the book of Acts all attest that the disciples believed Jesus rose from the grave, and that they saw Him afterwards on numerous occasions. People want to discount these accounts, but it is well accepted amongst scholars that all four gospels were written during the first century, at the most 70 years after Jesus walked the earth.

"Finally," Marcus continued, "early writings from the church leaders talk of the disciples witnessing Jesus after the resurrection. Many of these early church fathers were disciples of the disciples. People such as Clement, Irenaeus, and

Polycarp wrote about the resurrection and the disciples' proclamation of this event. Polycarp himself mentioned the resurrection five times in his letter to church in Philippi around 110 AD."

"So, you are saying because the disciples believed Jesus rose from the dead that's evidence for the resurrection actually taking place?" I asked.

"It's just one of the evidences, Wyatt," Marcus said. "Remember, just as there are different pieces of the puzzle of why I believe in God and specifically Jesus Christ, there are pieces of the puzzle pointing to the historicity of the resurrection. The evidence that the disciples claimed and believed Jesus rose from the dead is one of those pieces. Backing up this claim that they believed Jesus rose from the dead is the evidence of their changed lives, and the fact that the disciples were willing to die for this claim."

"Yes, but don't other people in history die for their beliefs?" I asked.

Marcus nodded. "Yes, this is true, but here is the distinction. People are willing to die for beliefs in something they believe is true but are not eyewitnesses to those beliefs. The disciples were eyewitnesses to the risen Christ, as they claimed. If they made this up, would they be willing to be tortured and die for a lie?"

I said nothing but felt my mind and heart stirred by Marcus' logic and words. I remember Peter, when led to the cross, said he was unworthy to be crucified like his Lord, so they hung him upside down. Through all that, he refused to recant his claim that Jesus had arisen.

Marcus looked at me. "Do you have any questions, Wyatt, before I continue?"

"No, go ahead."

"Okay. Let's look at the amazing change that took place in Paul who was a leading persecutor of the early church. A Pharisee, he also held the coats of those who stoned Stephen to death. Paul's life was forever changed, however, on the road to Damascus, where on his way to arrest more followers of Jesus, he encounters the risen Christ. This experience recorded in Acts, and talked about in his letters, causes a dramatic change in Paul. Over time, he became the traveling apostle, sharing the evidence of the risen Christ from his personal encounter."

Marcus picked up a puzzle piece. "Then there's James, the brother of Jesus. Early in the Gospels, it talks about how James doubted Jesus in both Mark and John. However, in Paul's letter to the Corinthians, he says that, among others, Jesus appeared after His resurrection to James. In Acts it later says that James was a leader in the early church and later died as a martyr. His martyrdom is attested to in the New Testament as well as other historical, non-Christian sources, such as Josephus."

"So why are the changes in Paul and James strong evidence for the resurrection?" I asked.

"Because of the dramatic change in both of their lives, and the fact both were eyewitnesses of the resurrected Jesus," Marcus said. "And, like the other disciples, they both died for their claims. Neither were willing to recant their belief in the risen Christ to save their own lives. It's evidence something powerful did happen in their lives."

Marcus looked directly at me, eyes earnest. "And now, the most compelling evidence for the resurrection, the empty tomb."

Marcus shifted in his chair and smiled at me. "Wyatt, the

evidence for the resurrection really shows itself when examining the evidence for the empty tomb and the physical appearances of Jesus after the resurrection. Skeptics such as Josh McDowell, Lee Strobel, and Frank Morison became believers after examining this evidence."

"Who are they?" I asked.

"Good question," Marcus said. "McDowell was a brilliant college student and atheist who set out to disprove Christianity and silence his believing friends. His research had the opposite effect, especially the evidence for the resurrection. Strobel was a Chicago crime reporter for the *Chicago Tribune* whose wife became a follower of Jesus. He also set out to disprove Christianity and from his research discovered the belief was based on historical evidence that compelled him to turn his life over to Christ. And Frank Morison wrote the classic *Who Moved the Stone* in 1930 after his own pilgrimage brought him to the realization that the resurrection had compelling evidence to its historicity."

"So, what exactly is the evidence shown from the empty tomb?" I asked. The combination of the topic and Marcus' obvious enthusiasm caught my attention.

"Glad you asked." Marcus' smiled. "In all four Gospels, the empty tomb is reported. Interestingly, women were the first to witness the empty tomb and the first appearance of Jesus. If this story were made up by the disciples, historians agree it would be silly for them to have women as the first to witness the event since, in that culture, women's views were not taken seriously. The fact that the Gospels share that those women were the first to witness the empty tomb and then shared the remarkable event with the disciples underscores the event's authenticity."

At this point I interrupted. "But don't the gospel accounts of the empty tomb differ? I remember reading in one Gospel it was just two Mary's that discovered the empty tomb, while in another, three are mentioned. In another, more women are mentioned. One Gospel has Mary Magdalene meeting Jesus at the empty tomb, and another doesn't mention any of the women seeing Jesus. One Gospel has an angel sitting on the large rock that was rolled away from the tomb, while another says two men were inside the tomb. Don't all these inconsistencies show a lack of confidence in the resurrection?"

Marcus looked at me and nodded. "Very good, Wyatt. I see you have been doing some reading. However, I would counter your conclusion. Instead of causing doubt, the differing accounts actually add credibility to the resurrection and empty tomb account."

"How so?"

Marcus smiled. "Let's say you take me and a couple of your other friends to a Kansas City Chiefs football game. The four of us go to the same game, watch the whole game together, then drive back home. When each of us are asked about the game, do you think we are going to tell it the same way?"

"Well, no, not exactly," I admitted.

Marcus laughed. "Of course not! You might talk about how good the offense played. I might talk about how good that hot-dog was! One of your friends might talk in detail about the final minutes of the game, and the other friend focuses on the crowd. Each of us was a witness to the same game, but our takes were a little different. Did any of us make up our stories?"

I smiled. "No, Marcus."

"That's right!" Marcus patted my knee. "Another example. A detective investigates a robbery at a bank. He interviewed four witnesses to get their eyewitness account of what happened. A detective looks for collaborative testimony. In other words, if witnesses tell the same story, the detective suspects a rehearsed testimony. Collaborative testimony lines up what happened, but what each witness recounts isn't the same, even the physical description of the robber."

Marcus leaned closer to me. "So it is with the Gospels. If the Gospels shared the eyewitness events of the life of Jesus and His resurrection in exactly the same way, it would cause one to think of a rehearsed, made-up story. However, the differences, while not being contradictory but expressed differently by the gospel writers, shows more authenticity to historians. Does that make sense, Wyatt?"

I nodded. "Actually, it does."

My heart stirred again. Not only were Marcus' words logical and convincing, but his calm yet passionate approach seemed to be blowing heat into the long-cooled embers in my soul.

Marcus continued. "Now there have been many explanations of what happened to the body of Jesus. Some claimed the disciples stole the body. One of the Gospels mentioned this rumor started by the religious leaders, telling the guard to say this happened. However, if the disciples stole the body of Jesus, that means they were proclaiming a known lie. Why were their lives suddenly changed? Why were they willing, and most did, to die for a lie? It just doesn't make logical sense.

"Another theory, called the swoon theory, claims Jesus didn't actually die on the cross and later woke up. This theory has many problems. For one, the evidence for His death when the spear went through His side and water and blood both came out. Secondly, even if He did wake up in the tomb, how would He, in his very injured state, move the large stone and get past the guards?"

"True, and if he was just a man, it seems the authorities would eventually find him, capture him, and announced this in history," I said.

"Good point, Wyatt! Another theory is about the tomb. People have speculated that the authorities moved the body to a different tomb. The logical problem with that theory is once the disciples claimed Jesus rose from the grave, why didn't they simply produce the body and end the movement? Another similar theory states the women went to the wrong tomb, which seems implausible. But even if they did, once again, the authorities could have produced the body. The fact they didn't points to the evidence the body was gone."

Marcus leaned forward and continued. "The appearances of Jesus after the resurrection have to be accounted for. The Gospels, Acts, and Paul's letter in First Corinthians show that Jesus appeared to the disciples more than once, to James the brother of Jesus, to Mary Magdalene and other women, and to over five hundred people at one time. These appearances occurred over a period of several weeks before Jesus ascended to the Father, according to Acts."

"Could the appearances of Jesus have been made up in later years and reported as fact?" I asked.

"Legend is what you are referring to, and skeptics have proposed this explanation for the resurrection and the appearances of Jesus after the resurrection, but it just doesn't hold up."

"Why?"

"Because of the early eyewitness accounts and Paul's words in First Corinthians 15, historians refer to as one of the oldest creeds of the early church, maybe dating as early as 32 to 38

AD, as early as two to eight years after the resurrection. Also, if the appearances were merely legendary, that still doesn't explain the empty tomb. You have to take the evidence of the empty tomb and the appearances into account together," Marcus said.

I nodded. That made sense. "Are there any other attempts at explaining the appearances of Jesus?" I asked.

"Yes," said Marcus. "There have been those who proposed mass hallucinations, since Jesus appeared before several disciples together, as well as over five hundred at one time. Psychologists will tell you that hallucinations are an individual phenomenon. They simply do not occur with groups of people. Also, in John 21, Jesus cooks and eats with the disciples on the shore. In another appearance, He had Thomas touch His nail scars to prove His resurrection."

I agreed with Marcus' take on it. "Yeah, the hallucination theory seems very unlikely."

Marcus smiled. "Indeed. So, when you put all these pieces together of the resurrection, I believe the most likely explanation is something quite remarkable happened that changed the course of history. The disciples, who at one time had fled the scene and were hiding out in fear for their lives, suddenly boldly proclaimed that Jesus had risen and were willing to die rather than recant this belief. Paul, who at one time was arresting followers of Jesus, suddenly became a follower and wrote most of the letters of the New Testament after seeing the risen Savior. The evidence for the resurrection is compelling and reasonable in light of the evidence, in my opinion."

Driving home after my long visit with Marcus, I reflected on our conversation. My faith of the past had all been about church ritual and being with my grandmother. I had never deeply researched its roots and evidence. I thought faith was a blind belief. To doubt was to sin. In my conversations with Marcus, I realized that faith was not blind but reasonable and full of vision and clarity when investigated and thought through. Faith was about believing not just with our hearts but also with our minds.

I had a lot to think about.

19

Marcus' Past Pieces

"I'd sure like to see my old home before I leave this world," Marcus said as we chatted about a week after my last visit. He sat working on his same puzzle, about halfway through it.

"What is the name of the town you grew up in?" I asked.

"Oak Creek," Marcus said. "I'd guess about thirty minutes outside of Russellville. It would probably be about five hours from here."

"I'll take you," I said, surprised by my sudden offer.

"Oh, no. That's too far a drive, Wyatt. I appreciate it, though."

I persisted. "No, I like taking trips. We can make a day of it. How about I pick you up this Saturday at about seven a.m. after I check with my wife, and we'll head down that way. We can eat lunch there, look for your old home, drive around your old town, then head back by evening."

Marcus smiled. "Well, now. I'd sure like that. Are you sure, Marcus?"

"You bet I am!" I said. "It will be a fun adventure!"

I checked with the nursing home staff, got their permission, and talked to Mary, who thought it very sweet of me to do this for Marcus. I showed up the following Saturday a couple of minutes before seven a.m. Marcus stood outside the door using a walker, smiling and nodding as I drove up. I rolled my window down, and he quickly walked to the passenger side.

"Are you ready for our adventure?" I asked.

"Absolutely!" Marcus said.

I helped fold and place his walker in the back seat of my 2007 Pontiac Vibe. The car had over 250,000 miles on it but still ran like new.

We got on the road and started our journey to Marcus' hometown. Marcus smiled as we drove, excited to be going to his boyhood home and getting away from the nursing home for a day. The air felt hot and heavy from the Ozark Mountain summer air, but my air conditioning still worked well.

As we drove, Marcus told story after story of growing up in Oak Creek. He shared about catching crawdads in the creek with his brothers, fishing for catfish, and evenings on the porch, listening to the sounds of the night. I drove in silence, listening to my friend relay stories about his life, happy to share a new memory with him.

We arrived at Oak Creek and stopped at a local barbecue restaurant for lunch. Marcus recalled his friends who used to own the place that had a different name when he was younger.

"Oh yeah, Jimmy's Red-Hot BBQ!" he said. "They had the best ribs. Meat fell right off the bone!"

After lunch, we drove around the town. Marcus would share stories about the various businesses, surprised everything was pretty much the same, except older and more run down. Marcus kept shaking his head, sad to see his old town looking so rusted and weary.

"Kind of like me," he said.

"You're not run-down, Marcus!" I said. "You are the wisest man I've ever met. You've still got lots of life in you!"

Marcus smiled. "Well, thank you, Wyatt. I haven't had too many white folks tell me that over the years. That means a lot."

"So, racism was pretty bad down here?" I asked.

"Oh yeah. Growing up around here I would say it was about eighty percent white, twenty percent black. As I got older, more and more folks from Mexico moved up here, and they weren't treated very well either."

I stared at Marcus' sad eyes. It made me ashamed of my past feelings of superiority over folks of color. I learned this from my dad and friends of my dad, and as I thought about it, even from my mom.

"Do you have any bitterness about how you were treated?" I asked.

Marcus sighed. My car now sat in the small, quiet downtown square. Many buildings stood vacant.

"I have given my anger and bitterness over to the Lord a long time ago, Wyatt, but I have to admit, the old bitterness does creep up from time to time as I hear stories of racism still happening today. I just have to keep giving it to the Lord."

I noticed a single tear rolling down Marcus' cheek.

"I've had to battle over the years, Wyatt," Marcus continued, looking straight at me. "I remember white folks moving out of our neighborhood because we and another black family lived there. I was rejected from several colleges because of the color of my skin. I got passed over promotion after promotion when I was a professor I believe because of the color of my skin. Even in God's church white folks would sit in the front pews and us black folks sat in the back. It's just shameful." Marcus shook his head.

We drove up to his childhood home, now long vacant.

Windows sat broken, and the roof showed many missing shingles, caved in slightly on the western side of the house. We walked up to the front door and checked to see if it was locked. It wasn't.

We carefully opened the door and walked in. Trash was scattered across the living room floor. Graffiti was spray-painted across the walls. Marcus remained quiet as we walked from room to room, careful about where we stepped, gently pushing himself along with his walker. Marcus showed me the room he grew up in and shared with two of his brothers. A tiny bathroom sat in the middle of the home, which also served as their tornado shelter. Furniture was long gone from the house. Marcus wondered who owned the property and why the property still stood, obviously long past being inhabitable.

We stepped around the back to the small backyard. Marcus walked up to a large oak tree and smiled.

"My brothers and I used to climb this tree when it was smaller and have acorn fights." He rubbed his forehead. "I got several nice bruises from my brothers up here from acorns," he said with a chuckle.

We went from his childhood home to a café in the small downtown area. Marcus looked around at the pictures on the walls of local high school sports teams.

"I remember playing baseball and basketball in high school," he said. "I was in one of these pictures way back when."

"Were you good?" I asked.

"I was better at baseball. A little too uncoordinated for basketball. I played third base. I had a pretty good arm and hit well. My baseball coach was one of the few in our school who treated us all equally on the team, whether black or white. I looked up to Coach West."

I looked at Marcus and hesitated.

"What is it, Wyatt?" he asked, noting my eyes.

"Well, I was just wondering if it's hard for you to still believe in God sometimes with all your past hurt. Why would a loving God create beings who hate each other just because their skin color is different?"

Marcus stared at me for a moment without answering. Finally, he sighed.

"Yes, Wyatt, it is difficult sometimes to see God through the pain of hate and rejection, but then I remember that the same thing happened to Jesus when He walked this earth over two thousand years ago. Through it all, He was able to keep His eyes on the Father. With His help, I figure I can do the same."

We set out after our early dinner at the café for home. We rode in silence for many miles, except for the music on the radio that was a jazz station Marcus found. He smiled and hummed to some of the tunes. I noticed him tapping his knees with his fingers.

Suddenly Marcus spoke.

"Wyatt, I sure appreciate you bringing me on this trip. I know your wife needs you at home. Would you thank her as well?"

"Sure," I said. "She was glad I got to take you."

"She's a sweet one."

"Yes, she is. I'm a lucky man."

"A blessed man," Marcus corrected me.

The late afternoon sun painted a bright orange spread to the left of my vision as we made our way north. I reflected on our talk on beauty and design and felt a warm place in my heart that had been cool for so long. Marcus stared at the thickening sunset as well and smiled.

"Sure is a gorgeous day," he said.

"Yes, it is, Marcus."

I dropped Marcus off and headed home, noticing a full moon lighting my way home. I reflected on my day with Marcus. Seeing his childhood home and hearing his stories, good and bad, gave me a new understanding and appreciation for the man I found myself growing to love. It occurred to me that just as Marcus was helping me understand the reality of God via puzzle pieces, I was getting to know Marcus on a deeper level via the puzzle pieces of his life. Along with that, I was taking the time to find and observe different pieces in my life as well. Some of the pieces I rediscovered brought shame, such as my racist past and present.

My puzzle still had many pieces left to find and fit.

20

The Disciples' Piece

"I want to meet Marcus," Mary said as we enjoyed a Saturday morning breakfast together. Two weeks had passed since our trip to Marcus' hometown, and I missed my friend.

"So, you want to go with me today?" I asked.

"Yes, if that's okay with you?"

I smiled. "Of course. Marcus has been wanting to meet you. He'll be excited!"

Soon after, Mary and I set out for the nursing home. Mary's health had improved dramatically in the past month. Her recent tests showed the cancer had shrunk significantly. The light in her face glowed brightly again, bringing joy and relief to my heart.

Marcus grinned as we stepped toward him in his usual spot. "Well, who do we have here!" he said, standing from his wheelchair gingerly.

"Oh, you don't have to get up," Mary said while quickly offering her hand to Marcus' arm.

"Oh, yes I do!" Marcus said. "I want to hug you, Miss Mary!"

The two embraced while I watched, smiling. Marcus laughed as he sat back down in his chair, motioning for us to join him.

"I'm so excited you came, Mary," Marcus said. "How are you feeling this morning?"

"Really good," she said, sitting close to him. I quickly followed next to her.

"How's your puzzle coming?" I said, noticing he was getting closer to completion.

"I might get this blasted thing done by the end of the year, if the Lord don't take me first!" he said.

We all laughed. I could tell Marcus was taken with Mary. I smiled, looking at them both, feeling pride for my wife. Her beauty showed inside and out as she chatted with Marcus.

After a while, Marcus looked at me. "Wyatt, would you like to examine another piece of my puzzle today?"

"Sure," I said. "Mary wanted to not just meet you but hear some of our ongoing discussion."

"Good!" Marcus said, looking now at Mary. "I've enjoyed my talks with your husband, Mary, and I'm glad you get to join us today."

"I am too," Mary said, patting Marcus' arm.

Marcus picked up a piece and shook it gently in his hand. "Today we will look at the piece of the changed lives of Jesus' disciples after His resurrection."

Marcus shifted in his chair. "It's really amazing to see the change in these men who just a few days before had fled the scene when Jesus was arrested. Peter, the brash leader of the group, had boldly predicted he would never leave Jesus. Jesus countered that Peter would deny him three times before a rooster crowed. This all came to pass."

Marcus sat the puzzle piece down on the table. He took a sip of his coffee before continuing.

"But we read in Acts that after the resurrection and after witnessing Jesus risen from the grave, the disciples became a changed group. In hiding before, fearful of being found and arrested and possibly killed themselves, these same men boldly proclaimed the resurrection of their leader. Peter challenged the religious leaders. Before he denied even knowing Jesus but Peter now boldly proclaimed the miracle of the resurrection."

"Didn't they die for their belief that Jesus had risen rather than recant their claim?" Mary asked.

Marcus smiled. "Yes, indeed. That is so true. Early church fathers said Peter even asked not to be crucified like Jesus, saying he was unworthy to die the same way. So, they crucified him upside down. This same one who denied even knowing Jesus, trying to save his own skin, now boldly suffered and died for the resurrected Christ."

Marcus continued. "Understand this, the disciples of Jesus gained nothing from an economic standpoint in sharing the message of the resurrected Jesus. They faced a life of hardship. They were beaten, imprisoned, and lived on the run. What possible advantage would they have proclaiming a lie?"

"But what about those who follow cults and have died for what they believed to be true?" I asked. "What about Muslims and those who followed Jim Jones? Didn't they die for their beliefs?"

"Ahh, but there is a distinction, Wyatt," said Marcus. "People will die for their beliefs if they believe with their whole heart those beliefs are true, but people will not die for their beliefs if they know their beliefs are false. The disciples were willing to die for something they had seen with their own eyes and touched with their own hands. They all claimed to have seen the resurrected Jesus. If they had made this up, it would be highly unlikely that all the disciples would be willing to die for this lie, or in the case of John, be cast away on a remote island in isolation for his remaining days."

Mary smiled. "I see why Wyatt has enjoyed talking with you, Marcus! You are very wise."

Marcus shook his head. "No, I'm not wise. Just old!" He chuckled. "Lord knows I've been able to read a lot in my years. The more I read and study, the more my heart is settled on Jesus being the picture that shows up when you put all the pieces together."

Mary put her hand on Marcus' hand. "I want to thank you for caring so deeply for my husband these past few months. You have no idea how you have helped and impacted him." Her voice cracked.

Marcus put his other hand on top of hers. "It is my pleasure. Wyatt has become a dear friend. Goodness, he takes me places outside of here and puts up with all my stories and such!"

I looked at them both and smiled. "I should have brought you here sooner, Mary. I think Marcus is taken with you!"

We all chuckled as Mary wiped tears from her eyes.

Marcus picked up another puzzle piece. "The original disciples' lives were not the only ones who were changed dramatically after Jesus' resurrection. Paul, a successful Pharisee who arrested many followers of Jesus, gave it all up after a dramatic encounter with the risen Jesus. He became the main writer of the letters in the New Testament and the most prolific evangelist of the early church. Paul's life took such a dramatic turn because of Jesus physically appearing before him and calling Paul to follow Him. Paul later was killed for following Jesus. He would not recant."

Marcus put the piece down and picked up another. "James, the brother of Jesus and at one time His critic, became the early leader of the church and was one of the first martyrs for following Jesus. His life also changed dramatically when Jesus appeared to him after His resurrection. All these dramatically changed lives after the resurrection of Jesus point toward something powerful that happened to cause this change. Another piece of the puzzle for why I believe what happened really happened. Jesus rose from the dead, culminating His message to pay the penalty for our sin, then rose in victory over death, thus paving the way for us who believe to conquer death too someday!"

Marcus smiled while shaking the puzzle piece. Mary also smiled. I nodded, sensing renewed faith mixed strangely with deep sadness and anger. Broken parts in my past seemed to be at the root of my dark emotions. Why couldn't my parents have had a significant change in their lives?

21

Time with Mom

I spent the week stewing over Mary and my conversation with Marcus about the changed lives of the disciples. My anger and frustration confused me at the end of our time together. Mary could tell I was struggling but left me alone with my thoughts. After a few days, I decided my anger rooted itself deep down in my wounds growing up and the hypocritical picture of Christianity I witnessed at home and in our church.

I decided early the following Saturday morning to visit my mom. I hadn't talked with her in a couple of weeks and felt guilty for not checking on her more, especially since we lived only twenty minutes from her. Perhaps a visit with her would help with my anger. I didn't know.

Mom worked at the local grocery store over the past ten years. I knew she was off Saturday mornings and liked to smoke and watch birds on her front deck. Sure enough, as I drove up there, she sat, staring at me as I got out of my car.

"Hi, Mom," I said as I stepped up on the deck.

"Hello, Wyatt. How are you and Mary?"

"We're good. Mary has been feeling much better lately."

"Well, that's good." I could tell she seemed hurt.

I sat next to her, trying to stay away from her smoke. Mary was allergic to smoke, so I didn't want to bring the smell home.

"I'm sorry I haven't called or come by lately," I said. "It's been really busy at work."

"That's okay," she said, taking a puff of her cigarette and gently tapping it on her ashtray.

"What have you been up to?" I asked.

She sighed. "Oh, just work and sitting here. Not much else going on."

I looked at Mom's hand holding the cigarette. I could see it was shaking. The hands looked older than her fifty-something years, and her eyes had brown patches under them.

Ever since Dad left, Mom retreated into herself, not spending much time with family or others outside her work circle. She didn't go to church either. Our visits and phone calls were sporadic at best. It seemed I always had to be the one to initiate.

"I don't think I told you about my friend, Marcus, I've been visiting at the nursing home."

"How did you meet him?" Mom asked.

"I met him several months ago while visiting Grandma. He's a retired Bible professor from Arkansas."

"Hmm," Mom said, taking another puff.

"He's a very nice man. At first, I didn't know how to take him. He's also black, which I'm not used to."

"No, there aren't too many black people around here, that's for sure," Mom said, looking at me with a half-interested expression.

"True. But as I've gotten to know him, I'm discovering he is one of the most amazing men I've ever met. He is so wise and caring. I took Mary to see him the other day. They took right to each other."

"Mary could get along with anybody, Wyatt. She's got that gift."

I smiled. "Yes. Yes, she does."

I stared at my mother. I saw such fatigue and defeat in her eyes. It broke my heart. True, I still struggled with unpleasant feelings toward her and especially Dad for how they treated us growing up. I never heard the words "I love you" from either of them but instead heard many terms of ridicule and verbal abuse.

However, looking at this woman I spent my childhood with, I couldn't help feeling deep empathy and sadness for her. I never heard much about her childhood other than poverty and a drunken father. I also know her marriage to Dad brought her sadness and regret, for Dad never invested in any of us much when he was around.

"How's work?" Mom asked while taking another puff.

"We've been swamped lately," I said. "I'm hoping to get a promotion soon."

"That would be nice." Mom flicked a long ash off her cigarette. "I'm sure you and Mary could use the extra money."

"How are you doing, Mom?" I tried to make eye contact with her. "I mean, really. You seem kind of down."

Mom sighed. "I'm just tired, Wyatt. I haven't been sleeping great, and work has been getting harder at my age. I just get tired of doing the same old thing each day." She sighed again, not looking me in the eyes.

"I'm sorry to hear that, Mom. Mary and I need to have you over for dinner soon. I'll check with her. What's a good evening for you?"

"Oh, you don't have to do that, Wyatt. I'm okay."

I put my hand on Mom's, suddenly feeling great love for her, which surprised me. "No, really. We want to spend more time with you."

Mom pulled her hand back quickly and looked away. "I

don't want to put you and Mary out. I know she needs to reserve her energy."

"She's feeling better, Mom. How about this Thursday evening? I'll confirm with Mary but am sure that will be good for both of us."

"We'll see," Mom said. "I do appreciate the invite, though."

I dropped the subject and sat back in my chair, wondering at the depth of Mom's hurt. While my dad was blessed with a great mom in Grandma Mabel, my mother's relationship with her mom and dad was always a mystery to us. She grew up with two older brothers in rural McDonald County, three counties west of our Taney County. Her dad was a truck driver, rarely home. Her mom stayed home with the kids and raised a garden, some pigs, and chickens. Mom rarely talked about her parents. I barely knew them. Her dad died of a heart attack when I was a kid, and her mother passed away from lung cancer when I was a teenager. Mom did spend a lot of time taking care of her those last few months, but she seemed even more distant after the funeral.

My thoughts were interrupted by Mom's words. "Do you want some lemonade?"

"Sure, that sounds good."

Mom slowly got up and entered the house, soon returning with a tall glass.

"Thanks," I said, watching Mom sit back down in her chair.

"When do you and Mary plan on having kids?" Mom asked.

I sighed. It seemed Mom asked this question almost every time I visited her. "We're not sure. We definitely want to wait until she is free and clear of cancer."

"Of course," Mom said, nodding. "It would really be hard

on her to be pregnant now. How many kids would you like to have someday?"

"We're thinking two to three. I'd love to have at least one boy and one girl."

Mom smiled. "Yes, that would be nice. I think you and Mary would be good parents, Wyatt."

"Why do you think that?" I asked, surprised by the compliment.

"You're both good people. Better than your dad and me, that's for sure." Mom looked away. I could see her eyes were glistening.

I put my hand on Mom's shoulder. "Mom, you had it rough raising us with Dad's drinking problem. You did the best you could."

She nodded, sniffing. "It was hard for sure. Your dad just seemed to give up after a while. I'm not sure why. I guess the alcohol consumed him."

"Us three boys weren't always easy either," I said, smiling. "We fought a lot and I'm sure drove you crazy!"

Mom chuckled. "Oh yes! Sometimes I just had to chase you out of the house for a while and lock the screen door to get some peace! Remember that?"

"Yep! For us it just meant more time to play outside!"

Mom smiled and looked at me. I could see the fatigue but also a glimmer of happiness reflecting on times with her sons.

"Did you go to church growing up?" I asked Mom, suddenly interested in exploring where she stood with God.

"Yes, off and on. Mom usually took us. Dad didn't go to church much that I remember, except on Easter."

"So was your mom pretty religious?"

Mom took a sip of her coffee. "I think she was. She didn't

talk much about the Bible or God with us, but I do remember seeing her read her Bible many mornings as we were getting ready for school."

I hesitated, looking at Mom. "How is your relationship with God, Mom?" I asked.

Mom was silent. She slowly shook her head. "I'm not sure, Wyatt. So much has happened with your dad and life . . . and losing Sharon. I do believe in God and the Bible, but I have not been going to church since your father left us and have not read the Bible much lately. I know I should go to church and pray more but just haven't."

"I understand, Mom. I've been struggling with my faith too lately."

"Why is that?" Mom asked, looking at me now with concerned eyes.

I leaned back in my chair and sighed. "I guess life has been so hard and unfair. Dad leaving, Sharon dying, and Mary's cancer. If God is real, why does He allow such suffering for us? I mean, it's not like we're evil and hurting others!"

My words tumbled out with more emotion than I planned. My voice started shaking, so I stopped and looked away.

I heard Mom's voice speak slowly. "Wyatt, we both need to not blame God for bad things that happen in life. It's because of sin, not God."

I looked at Mom with surprise. Her words, simple and to the point, made sense.

"That man at the nursing home has been helping me sort things out," I said.

"Good. He sounds like a wise man, Wyatt."

"Yes. Yes, he is," I said, smiling.

We chatted for another half hour or so, talking about how the brothers were doing, how Mom's small garden was faring, and if the Cardinals were going to be any good this year in baseball. I gave Mom a longer-than-normal hug before leaving, feeling our relationship experienced some healing in our time together. I'm not sure how it happened, but I left glad and grateful. It seemed this broken piece of my puzzle was slowly mending and fitting back into place. I knew it would take time and more effort on my part.

22

Changed Lives Piece

I walked into the nursing home entrance, ready for another visit with Marcus. A week had gone by since my encouraging time with my mother. Many layers of hurt feelings melted away during our conversation that day. A considerable weight seemed to have been lifted from my soul.

Marcus wasn't in his usual spot at his puzzle table. I noticed his puzzle was left in place. I asked a nurse tending to another patient if she knew where Marcus was. She said, most likely in his room.

I walked into Marcus' room for the first time. There Marcus lay reading his Bible. He looked up at me and smiled.

"Well, hello there, Wyatt! So good to see you!"

"Hello, Marcus. I was worried when I didn't see you at your usual spot."

Marcus put down his Bible. "Well, I didn't sleep great last night, so I decided to take an after-lunch nap. Been up a little while reading the Good Book."

I pulled up a chair near his bed. "Are you up for a visit?"

"Sure! Sure! I always look forward to visits from you, Wyatt! Do you mind if we do so here? I'm still feeling a bit weary."

"Of course."

"Good. Good. Tell me, Wyatt, how is Mary?"

"She's doing well and said to tell you hi."

"Well . . . you tell her I said hi and want to see her again soon!" Marcus said.

"I'll do that. I had a good visit with my mother last week, Marcus. It may have been the first time we really talked in years."

Marcus patted my arm. "Good. I bet that was good for your heart."

I nodded. "Yes, it was. It makes me want to spend more time with her, getting to know her better and hearing her story, like you and I get to do together."

"I think that would be a good thing," Marcus said. "A good thing, indeed!"

I leaned forward in my chair closer to Marcus. "I really appreciate our talks, Marcus. They have been a big help to my struggling faith. I still have my doubts but am wanting to work through them with your help."

"I'd love that!" Marcus smiled. "I was just thinking of the next piece of my puzzle. Want to hear it?"

"That's why I'm here!" I said, nodding and smiling.

"Okay then," Marcus said, pushing himself up from his bed. "I want to sit in my chair over here if you'll help me up to chat."

Marcus slowly swung his bare feet out of his bed. I smiled at his polka-dot pajamas. I put my hand under his arm as he slowly rose from the bed. I gently helped him the few feet over to his comfortable chair, adjusting my small chair to face him.

Marcus leaned back in his chair and pulled the leg rest up. "There, that's better! Thank you, Wyatt. Now we can talk!"

I looked at Marcus and marveled at the simple joy he exuded. Here he sat in a nursing home, away from family, health slowly fading, but he was full of life.

I envied him.

Marcus spoke. "Now I don't have my puzzle pieces with me, but picture the piece we are going to talk about today. I call it changed lives in history. I know I've talked about Paul, but I want to start with him again if I may."

"Sure," I said. "You're the professor!"

"That I am!" Marcus said, chuckling. "Like my attire?"

We both laughed.

"Paul's history tells the story of a Pharisee who chased after the early followers of Jesus, arrested them, and threw them into prison. He held the cloaks of those who stoned Stephen to death. And it was on the road to Damascus where he planned on arresting more Christians that Acts tells of Jesus appearing before Paul. This event turned Paul's life upside down. He went from being an enemy of Christ to a primary advocate for Christ."

"So, you are saying the changed life of Paul is evidence of the reality of Christ?"

"Yes, I am, Wyatt. Again, this is just one of the pieces of why I believe, but to me it's a big piece when you travel throughout Christian history. We've already talked about the changed lives of the disciples. We are talking about Paul now, but we are going to briefly also look at the history of lives who have been changed by following Christ and see a pattern that speaks reality and validity to the Christian faith."

"So, you believe changed lives point to the reality of God?" I asked.

"Indeed!" Marcus said, nodding. "Changed lives are like seeds that germinate in the soul and produce a crop of fruit-bearing plants. The proof is in the fruit!"

I thought about what Marcus said and asked myself, *What is the fruit in my life?*

Marcus looked up toward the ceiling. "Let's see, what are some other examples of changed lives? Let's start with some of the early church fathers. Polycarp is one."

"Polycarp?" I said. "That's a strange name!"

Marcus chuckled. "Yes, it is. Polycarp was a follower of John, one of the disciples of Jesus. He played an important role in the early church in battling false teaching that broke out during the decades after the apostles, or disciples of Jesus, died, including John. Polycarp was willing to die for his belief in the risen Jesus rather than agreeing to burn incense to the Roman emperor. I have a quote from him on the day of his death. Let's see where I have it."

Marcus leaned over from his bed, pulled out a book, and thumbed through it. He stopped and pulled out a piece of paper.

"Here it is. This is what Polycarp said on the day of his death. "Eighty and six years I have served Him, and He has done me no wrong. How then can I blaspheme my King and Savior? You threaten me with a fire that burns for a season, and after a little while is quenched; but you are ignorant of the fire of everlasting punishment that is prepared for the wicked."

Marcus put the paper back in the book and placed it back on his nightstand. "It was written that they tried to burn Polycarp alive, but when the fire refused to consume him, they had to stab him to death to kill him. It was reported he never screamed out in terror or pain nor recanted his belief in Jesus, even to the end."

Marcus looked intently at me. "It takes a strong, unshakable belief to be willing to die like that, Wyatt. And throughout history, thousands of followers of Jesus were willing to die for their belief rather than recant. Either all those people were horribly deceived, or what they believed was true."

"What about the Muslim terrorists who were willing to die for their beliefs when they sent the planes into the World Trade Center and the Pentagon?" I asked.

"I believe they were horribly deceived," Marcus said. "They were committing acts of murder for their god. In studying all the pieces of my puzzle, that piece just doesn't fit."

I nodded. "Yes, I agree, but it's hard to also say because Christians are willing to die for their beliefs Christianity must be true."

"Remember, changed lives are just one piece of my puzzle," Marcus said. "You are right, Wyatt, it doesn't prove Christianity to be true. But it does give evidence, especially when you study many famous lives who have been changed and hear their stories. I think of Abraham Lincoln, Frederick Douglas, Dietrich Bonhoeffer, C.S. Lewis, Corrie Ten Boom, Martin Luther, and Martin Luther King. And there are many, many others whose stories point to dramatic life changes in following Christ."

Marcus shifted in his chair and coughed. "Excuse me. Think I got a little cold or something. I want to focus on a few changed lives that have encouraged my faith. C.S. Lewis was a brilliant mind who didn't believe in God. But after investigating the faith, Lewis became a believer and wrote the fantastic defense of his faith in the book *Mere Christianity.* Lewis, as you remember, talked in this book about the moral code I talked with you about awhile back, remember?"

"Yes, I remember," I said.

"Good! Well, I encourage you to read this book and hear more of Lewis' story. His specific journey of belief has been a piece of the puzzle of my own journey."

"Another man whose life story influenced me greatly was

George Washington Carver. Do you know much about him?"

"No, I can't say that I do," I said. "Didn't he have something to do with peanuts?"

"Yes!" Marcus laughed. He was a scientist in the 1930s who made over three hundred inventions using peanuts, especially peanut oil. He was a black man in a country full of racism, but his scientific mind and faith made him revered by both black and white America. His faith guided him throughout his life. When he was a week-old baby, he experienced racism in its purest form. George and his mother were kidnapped. The Carver family was able to ransom George, but his mother was never found. His dad had died before he was born, and years later, George was quoted as saying he 'started life as the orphaned child of a despised race.'"

Marcus shook his head and sighed. "Through all of this, Carver never gave in to bitterness. He said he accepted Christ at the age of ten and followed the Lord the rest of his life, teaching Bible studies for over thirty years. He never gave in to the allure of money and prestige. He turned down a high-salary job from Thomas Edison, feeling he was called to serve his people where he lived. Reading about his life, I was inspired to follow his example of not giving in to bitterness over how I was treated, and to keep my eyes on Jesus each day."

"Wow, he sounds like a brilliant man," I said.

"Yes, yes he was. And as intelligent and brilliant as he was, he believed in the God of the Bible. He is a piece of my puzzle, Wyatt."

Marcus looked tired. "Do you need to rest?" I asked. "We can continue this conversation another time if you want."

Marcus shook his head. "No, I'm fine. I'm enjoying this. I always enjoy our time together, Wyatt!" He reached over and patted my hand. "Let's see, who else has influenced me? There are so many . . . I know. Corrie Ten Boom! Have you heard of her?"

"Yes, she lived through the German concentration camps, correct?"

"That's right, Wyatt. I have read her book, *The Hiding Place*, many times. It is both a painful look at the evil of fallen man brought to full force as well as the power of love and faith in the face of evil. Corrie's sister, Betsie, who died in the concentration camp, showed Corrie supernatural faith by praying for their captors, even thanking God for their lice infestation, as it kept the cruel guards from entering their quarters and beating them. Betsie Ten Boom embodied Jesus' challenge to 'love your enemies' like few have."

"I can't imagine loving those who are torturing and killing you," I said.

Marcus nodded. "Yes, amazing love, indeed. I think about all the white folks growing up calling me names and calling me 'boy.' I must admit I did not show love toward them in my heart. No, I'm thankful for God's patience with me. Jesus on the cross showed this kind of love when He asked the Father to forgive those killing Him. He set the supreme example."

It was quiet for a few moments, each of us seemingly deep in our thoughts and memories. I thought about my dad and his abandonment of us. My heart still felt cold and hard toward him.

Marcus continued. "Other folks inspire my faith by their journey from atheism to becoming a follower of Jesus. I've mentioned Josh McDowell and Lee Strobel to you already in an earlier conversation. Remember, both were atheists who set out to disprove Christianity only to become followers of Jesus after their research led them to belief."

I typed notes of those two authors on my phone, determined to read their works. I looked at Marcus.

"I think I'm going to let you rest now, Marcus. I really appreciate your time today."

"My pleasure, Wyatt. I encourage you to examine the lives of many over the centuries who have put their faith in Christ. Many missionaries over the years have given their lives for their belief in the risen Savior. I think of Jim Elliot for one. He along with four other men were speared to death in Ecuador by an Indian tribe they were trying to befriend back in 1956. Amazingly, soon after Jim's widow, Elizabeth, returned to the same tribe with other widowed wives of the missionaries and led many to Christ. Jim was quoted once saying, 'He is no fool who gives what he cannot keep in order to gain that which he cannot lose.' It's one of my favorite quotes."

I noted Jim and Elizabeth Elliot's names on my phone, fascinated by their stories. I hugged my dear friend and walked out of his room. My mind was whirling from the stories I just heard of lives from the early days of Christianity to today impacted by the life, death, and resurrection of Jesus.

Why was my life not impacted more? This piece of my puzzle haunted me as I drove home.

23

It Rings True

After my last visit with Marcus, I started reading biographies of some of the men and women he had talked about. I looked online and found the book *Mere Christianity* by C.S. Lewis and decided to start with him. After ordering the book, I finished my Saturday morning coffee and got in my car. It was time for my now weekly visit with Marcus.

Marcus was sitting outside in a wheelchair when I arrived late in the morning. The early fall air felt crisp but warm on my face. Marcus had a small blanket on his lap and smiled as I approached.

"Good morning to you, Wyatt!"

"Good morning, Marcus. How are you feeling today?"

"Wonderful. Just enjoying God's sights and sounds!"

I found a plastic chair and pulled it up beside Marcus. Birds seemed to be singing in all directions, and the large maple tree gently swayed with the late morning breeze. The sun's filtering light danced with the pockets of shade on the lush grass underneath.

I sighed, taking in the sights and sounds with Marcus.

"How is Mary?" he asked.

"She's doing well. I took her to the doctor on Thursday, and he said that the cancer still appears to be in remission."

Marcus clapped his hands together. "Praise God! I'm so happy for you both!"

I smiled. "Thank you, Marcus. We are indeed happy and relieved."

Marcus patted my knee. "I have grown very fond of you both. Please give her my love and tell her I'd love to see her again soon."

"I will. She thinks a lot of you too."

For a few moments we sat soaking in the warmth of the sun and our own thoughts. Marcus finally broke the silence.

"We've looked at a lot of the pieces of my puzzle over the past few months, haven't we, Wyatt?"

I nodded. "We sure have. I've really learned a lot."

"Well, it's been good for me go over them again as well. In this broken world it's easy to forget the pieces when times are hard. I laugh about this place, Wyatt, but it gets depressing here some days. Seeing others forget who they are, all the dying . . . It gets to me sometimes."

Marcus suddenly shook his head, and I saw a tear roll down his cheek. I put my hand on his arm and patted it gently.

"I'm sorry, Marcus. I'm always seeking your wisdom and encouragement and don't spend enough time checking on how you're doing."

Marcus put his other hand on mine, resting on his arm. "That's quite all right, my son. These times with you are the highlight of my week. You just being here is deep encouragement."

"Have you heard from your family lately?"

"No . . . no, not for a awhile," Marcus said, his voice trailing off.

"I'm sorry, Marcus."

Marcus forced a weak smile. "It's okay. I know how busy they are with their lives. The last time I heard from each of them they seemed to be doing well. That makes me happy."

I felt sudden frustration and anger toward Marcus' kids. They had an amazing, engaging father, and they abandoned him here. Much like my father left me and my brothers, these kids had done the same with their father it seemed to me.

Marcus interrupted my thoughts suddenly. "I'd like to talk about one of the final pieces of my puzzle, Wyatt. It's an interesting piece. I call it, the truth rings true."

"Hmm . . . that's interesting, Marcus. What does that mean?"

He smiled. "Well, for myself, the story of the Gospel, from the time I heard it clearly, has always rung true to my heart. You know, there are many different beliefs about God, from Buddhism, Hinduism, Muslim to various other beliefs. But only in Christianity do we see the character of God as One who reaches down to us in love. This is both a fantastic and deep truth to me, Wyatt."

I hesitated. "Not to be disrespectful, Marcus, but that's not really evidence for belief. It sounds more like feelings."

Marcus nodded. "True, Wyatt. I concede I'm talking in part about emotions, but I believe deep truth resides more than just in the brain, but also the heart and soul. This piece of the puzzle I speak about now goes to the marrow of my bones. It comes from *experience* of faith, not just knowledge of faith."

"What do you mean?" I asked.

"I'm talking about seeing how my story fits into God's story and seeing how life just seems to ring true when I understand God's story from the Bible and how my life fits into it. The Bible talks about evil in the world and shows it. I've seen evil my whole life. The Bible talks about the whole earth being affected by the fall, the groaning of creation. I've seen this my whole life, from tornados to droughts. The Bible talks about God loving us and wanting to restore us. In my life, as I've followed Him and put my trust in Him, I've seen Him reshape my life from utter desolation to hope and joy."

I sighed. "For me I've had a hard time seeing God amid my family and my wife's cancer. The ring for me has not been true. It's been distant."

Marcus nodded slowly. "I understand, Wyatt. In this fallen world with all the noise of pain and busyness and confusion, it can be hard to see the ring of God's truth. Just remember, part of the truth is that it is a fallen world. For me, truly understanding and accepting that, instead of just blaming God for it, has helped me gather peace through the storms."

I quietly absorbed the words Marcus just shared. I stared at my old friend's weathered face, wondering what pain he must have endured over the years. Yet here he sat, full of faith, joy, and hope.

I envied him.

Marcus looked at me. "What are you thinking, Wyatt?"

I sighed. "Just thinking about your words. I'm wondering why my belief isn't as strong as yours, I guess."

"Remember, Wyatt. I'm a little older than you." Marcus smiled. "My faith has been a journey, with many peaks and valleys. I've been where you are at now, believe me."

I smiled. Those words helped. I knew that my doubts and struggles were not unique, but it helped to hear a man of such deep faith as Marcus share similar struggles in his journey. It lightened the load on my heart, giving me hope.

"I tell you what rings true for me the most about my faith, Wyatt," Marcus said. "Over the years, as I've made it a point to spend considerable time in the Gospels, I've sought to know in a deeper way the character of Jesus. In doing so, I believe I'm getting to know the character of God, as Jesus said when you see Me, you see the Father. Aspects of Jesus' character have drawn me deeper into my belief, giving my belief a firmer foundation."

"What aspects of His character in particular?" I asked.

Marcus rubbed his chin with his hand. "Well, now, let me think on that, Wyatt. Good question. For one thing, the way He cared for those in the culture who were marginalized. He touched a leper to heal him when you weren't supposed to get within six feet of them back then. He had a one-on-one conversation with a Samaritan woman. Back then men didn't talk with women in public like that, and the Jewish people didn't associate with Samaritans. But Jesus did."

A squirrel ran up the base of the large maple tree in front of us, stopping and starting often, looking around nervously. Marcus chuckled.

"That squirrel is like lots of folks today, busy scurrying around and always nervous about what others think of them. Jesus never worried about what others thought of him. His concern was pleasing His Father and caring for the needs of the people He met."

We both chuckled, watching the squirrel continue his nervous journey up the tree.

"Let me ask you, Wyatt, in your years hearing about Jesus and reading about Him, what stands out to you about him?"

"Hmm." I thought for a moment. "I remember liking how He treated the woman caught in adultery. He didn't shame her but forgave her, while encouraging her to leave her life of sin. He balanced grace and truth very well with people."

"Yes! Very good, Wyatt!" Marcus said. "Jesus showed great

compassion toward those who sinned but were sorry for their mistakes. A common short phrase Jesus' used with people He met was, 'Follow me.' Many of His disciples were called with this invitation, an invitation He offers to us all today."

I drove out of the nursing home parking lot and headed home, our conversation replaying in my thoughts. Why did the story of Jesus ring true for Marcus but not as much for me? Or did the story of Jesus ring true for me, but the message became clouded due to my broken life? Had I allowed weeds of bitterness to choke out the message? Why were my parents so messed up growing up? Why did my dad leave us? Why did my sister have to suffer so much and take her life? Why did my Mary have to suffer from cancer? Why haven't we been able to have kids yet?

So many questions. I suddenly wanted to talk out loud to God as I drove.

"Father, I know I have been distant from You, and to be honest, have doubted Your existence. I've been angry with You. I've seen so much pain and unfairness in my life. It's been hard. But I do thank You for putting Marcus in my life and showing me the truth of Your reality through his life and words. I still am struggling, though, with fully surrendering to You. Doubts still creep into me, and old wounds have not healed. Please show me in a clear way You are real, and that You really love me. I want to follow You like the disciples did, but I'm just not sure. I guess I'm afraid I will get hurt again. I don't know, God. I'm just confused. Please help me with this."

I drove on in silence. A strange sense of peace came over me as I turned into my driveway with the thought, "I have never left you," popping into my mind.

Mary greeted me with a big hug as I walked through the door, smiling.

"How was Marcus?" she asked, holding me close.

"He was good. We had another great talk."

"Good. I want to hear all about it, but first, I have something to tell you."

I looked at her and noticed her eyes suddenly well up with tears, although she was smiling.

"What is it? Is everything okay?"

"Everything is wonderful!" she said.

Mary pulled out of her pocket a small device that I didn't recognize at first. Suddenly it dawned on me.

It was a home pregnancy test.

24

Darker Pieces

"That is wonderful!" Marcus said while laughing with joy upon hearing the news of Mary's pregnancy. It was the day after Mary told me, and I had to return the following day, Sunday afternoon, to tell Marcus.

"Isn't it?" I said, beaming. "Mary hasn't stopped smiling since telling me!"

"Well, children are indeed a gift from God, Wyatt. You and Mary will make great parents, I'm sure."

"Thanks, Marcus. I know Mary will be an incredible mom. I hope I will be a good dad."

Images of my father crept into my mind. The fear of being like him with my own children sent a chill deep into my soul.

Marcus studied my face. "You know, Wyatt, with God's help, we can break the cycle of sin from our parents. I know you will be a great dad."

I looked down. "I hope so. I'm excited and overwhelmed at the same time." I marveled at how Marcus seemed to read my mind.

"As well you should!" Marcus chuckled. "As well you should."

"Do you remember what it was like being a dad for the first time?"

Marcus looked up into the sky. It was warm, but not a hot early afternoon. Sitting together under the shade of the big maple, the shaded breeze felt comfortable.

"Well, I'll tell you, Wyatt. I sure do. And like you, I was both excited and overwhelmed, and exhausted!" He chuckled. "A newborn doesn't have the same sleep cycle as you and me, that's for sure!"

I smiled but inside felt nervous about what lay ahead. The idea of me being a dad both excited and frightened me. Above all else, however, I felt gratitude that my wife was healthy now and pregnant.

Marcus stared at me, smiling. His face seemed to glow with joy. "You are entering a new and glorious chapter, Wyatt. I am so happy for you and Mary. But know that most likely, in this fallen world, the joy will be mixed with heartbreak and struggle. This child will bring you joy but also worry and, at times, heartache. Know that."

"Did you experience that as a dad?" I asked.

"I still do," Marcus answered. His smile suddenly vanished.

We didn't say anything for a couple of minutes. I sensed Marcus needed to gather himself. Then he sighed and looked at me.

"I want to talk about some other pieces of my puzzle, Wyatt. These are pieces honestly I'd rather not talk about."

"Why is that?"

Marcus looked up at the sky and sighed again. "Well, I call these pieces the darker pieces of my puzzle. These pieces are suffering, struggle, unfairness, and brokenness."

"Wow," I said. "I can see why you don't want to talk about these pieces. For me, these have been pieces of my puzzle of why I'm not sure I believe in God anymore."

"I know, Wyatt. While I don't like talking about it, that's why I feel it's important that we do. Dark pieces are a part of all our lives in this broken world. It's important to understand that, and why that is, and why these pieces ultimately point toward God."

"How do they point toward God?" I asked, frustration coming out unintentionally in my voice. "It seems they point away from God if He's all good and loving."

Marcus nodded. "Yes, you are right. Originally all evil and brokenness points away from God. Our broken world is a result of our rebellion from God starting with the original fall of Adam and Eve. Romans 3:23 says, 'All of us have sinned and fallen short of the glory of God.' However, Romans 8:28 says that 'for those who love God all things work together for good, for those who are called according to his purpose.' Notice in both verses the word all is used, Wyatt. That means all of us have sinned, causing more brokenness in this world; but God, for those who love Him, brings good from all things, even the broken things."

I shook my head. "That's just hard for me. How has God brought any good from my dad leaving our family? How has He brought good from my sister killing herself?" My voice shook.

Marcus put his hand on my knee and leaned forward. "Honestly, I don't know, Wyatt. God's good isn't just about us. It's about all of us. We see our own stories of brokenness, while God sees all our stories together as patchworks of His greater story. We might not see all the good He does through torn pieces such as your dad and sister, but if we believe and trust God's character, we can hold on to that."

"I don't know, Marcus . . ."

Marcus looked up again at the maple tree. "Wyatt, see this beautiful tree? Notice how the light filters in and out of the tree, but look at the dark areas where the light causes shadows. It is in the mixture of light and darkness that we get contrast and beauty. Artists use the contrast of light and darkness to produce great works of art. In the contrast of darkness and light is what produces meaning and beauty. Do you understand?"

I stared at the tree. "I guess so. Like you had told me earlier when we talked about beauty, without darkness and contrast you don't have beauty. If all were light it would blind us."

"Exactly," Marcus said. "If God were to make us without free will, we would have no choice. We would be programmed to do what God wants. There would be no evil, but there would be no love, because true love must be a choice. God did not create evil, but He created the possibility of evil by giving us free will. We brought evil into this world when we chose to rebel from God and go our own way. All the pain and brokenness of this world started with us in our free will choosing to go against God."

"So, all this pain is our fault?" I asked. "Is God not to blame? Why doesn't He stop it?"

"Yes, Wyatt. It's our fault. Also, Satan's fault, the great deceiver. We mustn't forget the cosmic battle going on between forces of evil and good. It's a two-layered problem."

"So, what does this have to do with the contrast of darkness and light?" I was confused.

"Good point, Wyatt. I'm going a bit all over the place. There's really a lot to cover with this topic. The bottom line is God promises to work all things for good. Like a great artist uses a variety of colors to bring about a beautiful work, I believe God uses all the good and bad of our lives to bring about His beautiful artwork of redemption. He does it in each of our lives, and in all our lives collectively."

"Can you give me an example in your life where God brought good from the evil in your life, Marcus?"

He put his hand over his chin and stroked his beard slowly, looking directly at me. "Hmm. That's a good question, Wyatt. Very good. That would be a good exercise for both of us to spend some time on. But as I'm thinking, one example comes to mind. I will tell you that God has used all the racist remarks directed at me to give me greater empathy for special needs folks. I remember seeing a person with cerebral palsy or down's syndrome and reaching out to them, knowing that they have endured hateful remarks due to their disability. I could have just been filled with anger and bitterness, but God gave me a more sensitive heart to others riddled with abuse or challenges in their lives."

I nodded. "Okay, that's a good example."

"You know what the greatest example is of God bringing His good from evil, Wyatt?"

"No, what?"

"It's Jesus on the cross. The Son of God coming to Earth and us putting Him to death on the cross. Satan appeared triumphant over the death of God's Son. But just as was predicted in Genesis when God said the serpent would bite Eve's seed in the heel, but the seed would crush the serpent's head, Jesus rose three days later. The ultimate good, our hope for eternal salvation, came from the ultimate bad, the death of Jesus. God illustrated Romans 8:28 in its purest form on this event."

"So, what would you say then is the ultimate answer to why God allows evil to remain in our world?"

Marcus answered, measuring his words. "I believe the answer . . . is Jesus Himself."

"What do you mean?"

"God's answer to our suffering is Jesus, who came to this world in His first physical visit as the suffering servant, taking all our suffering, pain, and sin upon Himself, and forever bonding those of us to Him who have put our trust in Him. His answer to our suffering is that He is right there with us in and through the suffering. Remember Jesus' words in John 16:33: 'In this world you have tribulation, but take courage; I have overcome the world.'"

For some reason, the words take courage resonated in my heart. In my personal battle with God through all my struggles and trials, I felt like instead of taking courage in God, I retreated into bitterness and dissolution. It also struck me that Jesus did not promise a rosy life for His followers. He promised that we would have struggles, trials, and pain, but to take courage in the fact that He overcame this world, ultimately via His resurrection from the dead. This should give us all great hope amid any struggle.

My heart stirred.

"Another reason why God still allows evil in the world," Marcus said, interrupting my thoughts, "is His patience and desire for more of us to return to Him."

Marcus pulled his Bible up from his lap and leafed through it.

"Here we go. Second Peter 3:9 says, 'The Lord is not slow to fulfill his promise as some count slowness, but is patient toward you, not wishing that any should perish, but that all should reach repentance.'"

Marcus looked at me with intensity in his eyes. "Wyatt, God could stop this world at any time with the snap of His fingers, but it says here it's His patience and desire that all of us reach repentance, that all of us return to Him and accept His forgiveness through Christ. We are a very impatient people. God is very patient."

I sighed. Patience was not one of my strong qualities, for sure.

"Here's another thought, Wyatt. People often ask, 'How could God bring something good out of the pain and evil in the world?' They seldom consider that without God the pain and evil are the final word. The reality is one is forced to accept one of two options on this: One, God can bring good out of brokenness even though we don't understand how, or two, brokenness, pain and evil will never be resolved or redeemed—they are the final word."

A cardinal landed on a lower branch close to us. Marcus and I both watched it and noticed a squirrel just a few branches further up, scurrying with a nut in his mouth.

Marcus leaned forward and put his hand on my shoulder.

"Wyatt, another piece of my puzzle that fits closely with these darker pieces we have discussed I call embracing the mystery."

"What does that mean?" I asked.

"Well, embracing the mystery is recognizing that, in this life we will not understand God totally, or have all our questions answered. To embrace the mystery is to learn to accept that fact, while still seeking to understand a little more each day."

"How does that help you believe in God more?" I asked, confused.

Marcus smiled. "Well, I think embracing the mystery helps us remember that God is so much greater than we are. We live in space in time in three dimensions. We have bodies that slowly break down. God is both inside and beyond space and time, is all-knowing, all-powerful, and ever present. He is the Alpha and Omega. He has no beginning and will have no end. To embrace the mystery is to accept a posture of humility toward who we are and who God is."

I was growing frustrated. "But I thought God wants us to know Him?"

"That is true, Wyatt. Jesus said eternal life is to know God the Father and himself. But I believe that is an eternal process. The joy of eternity will be knowing the God of unlimited knowledge more and more forever and ever!" Marcus almost yelled as he finished his sentence.

"That sounds all good for the future, Marcus, but what about now," I asked, my voice slightly shaking.

Marcus paused and looked at me. "Wyatt, I know your wounds are still deep and raw. I believe God understands and cares, but frankly he is more interested in your character than your comfort. He doesn't give us all the answers in this life because he's more interested in shaping our faith than our knowledge. Sometimes faith and knowledge go hand in hand. Sometimes faith stretches beyond what we can understand in the here and now."

I shook my head. "I'm having a hard time understanding this."

Marcus thought for a moment. "I read this once in a book by Dr. Hugh Ross. Let's imagine there is a universe out there that is only two-dimensional. All the beings in that universe are two-dimensional only with width and height, but not depth. Now let's say you as a three-dimensional being wanting to interact and reveal yourself to that two-dimensional world. How would you do it?"

"Hmm. I'm not sure."

Marcus pulled a pen and a small notepad from his shirt pocket. "Let me draw it out for you."

Marcus drew a box on the paper.

"This is the two-dimensional world. Now I as a three-dimensional being want to communicate with the two-dimensional world, so I enter their world. Now, what can beings in this two-dimensional world comprehend in myself? Let's say I stick one finger into their world. What will they see and perceive?"

I thought for a moment. "Only the two-dimensional part of me that intersects their world?"

"Exactly!" Marcus said. He then drew a small circle in the box. "The two-dimensional beings would only be able to comprehend this circle where my three-dimensional finger intersects their world. If I stuck three fingers through their world, they might think I'm three round beings. So, it is with a God who is beyond all dimensions intersecting our three-dimensional world when Jesus came to our earth. He's giving us a slice of understanding of who he is through the physical Jesus, a slice that is profound and life-changing, but just a small slice of his total being and character. That's why I say we need to embrace the mystery and appreciate how fantastic God is compared to ourselves. Does this make sense, Wyatt?"

I was stunned. The illustration suddenly made perfect sense. All my life, I had been trying to fit God into my sphere of understanding. This illustration showed me that it's okay for me not to totally understand God while living in this space and time world. Perhaps God revealed in Jesus is what I need to know in the here and now.

I drove home reflecting on my conversation with Marcus.

These dark pieces, I felt, were critical in my own puzzle. I had been doubting and struggling with God since childhood due to circumstances in my life, many of which seemed unfair. I thought again about my parents' unloving care for us, my sister's trauma and eventual suicide, my wife's battle with cancer, and my grandma's recent death.

"Father," I said out loud while staring at the approaching road, "I still have a lot of questions for You about why life is so hard and unfair."

My voice broke. Deep emotion came bubbling to the surface. Tears began streaming down my cheeks as I took a deep breath.

"I do thank You for Marcus, and the wisdom You have given him, and for putting him into my life. Help me to understand in a clearer way who You are and why You allow suffering while still being a loving God. I admit I still have my doubts, but I want to understand. I think I do believe, but please help my unbelief."

I drove the last few minutes home in silence, determined to forge ahead on this journey. The darker pieces, explained by Marcus, seemed to make the picture of reality clearer in my mind. It filled me with new hope.

25

Mom Meets Marcus

Mom rode with me in my car in silence. I could tell she was nervous by her jittery movements as we drove, frequently looking out her passenger window. I don't allow her to smoke in my car, which probably contributed to her nervous condition.

Over the phone, Mom mentioned she wanted to go with me to meet Marcus. I was shocked. I asked her why, and she said, "I've heard so much about him from you. I guess I want to meet him for myself." I knew Marcus would be very kind and gracious to Mom. I found myself uncertain about how Mom would react to Marcus.

I pulled the car into the parking lot, finding Marcus sitting outside by the maple tree, waving as we approached.

"Well, hello, Wyatt!" Marcus said. "And who do we have here?"

"Hi, Marcus. This is my mother, Sheila."

Marcus reached out his hand toward Mom, who leaned over and shook it gently. "It's sure a pleasure to meet the mother of this fine young man! Pleased to meet you, Miss Sheila."

"It's nice to meet you as well, Marcus. I've heard a lot about you," Mom said stiffly but politely.

We pulled up a couple of chairs next to Marcus' wheelchair. The morning air was cool and pleasant. The maple's leaves gently danced with the breeze.

Marcus looked at Mom. "Miss Sheila, thank you for coming with Wyatt today. I've been wanting to meet you."

Mom smiled slightly. "I've been wanting to meet you as well. I take it from Wyatt you and he have gotten to be pretty good friends."

"Oh, yes!" Marcus said, reaching forward and patting my knee. "My visits with Wyatt are the highlight of my week."

"As they are mine," I said. "You always give me a lot to think about after our conversations!"

Marcus chuckled. "Well, I hope I've been helpful on your journey, son."

"What kind of things do you two talk about?" Mom asked. I stared at her, surprised by the boldness of her question.

"Well, Miss Sheila," Marcus said, reaching into his shirt pocket, "we've been talking about puzzle pieces." He pulled out a small piece of the puzzle from his shirt.

"Puzzle pieces?" Mom said.

"Yes, ma'am. Puzzle pieces. To be more specific, how life and understanding why we are here are like pieces of a puzzle. When you look at these different pieces of life and how they fit together, it helps you understand and believe in the God who made us and loves us."

"Oh," Mom said, not smiling.

"If you don't mind me being so bold, Miss Sheila, may I ask if you believe in God?"

I sat silently, gazing at my mom. The directness of Marcus' question unnerved me, and I was worried Mom would bolt up from her seat and walk back to the car.

Instead, Mom looked away but answered quickly.

"I do, but I'm afraid I've strayed far from Him."

Marcus nodded. "We all have, Miss Sheila. The Bible says

all of us like sheep have gone astray. In this broken world, every one of us share in the brokenness. The fact of the matter is, we are all lost sheep in need of a Shepherd to come find us."

Mom looked now at Marcus. "I know. I know in my heart He's always been there for me. I think I've allowed my own bitterness to crowd him out."

Marcus nodded. "Oh yes, I've been there, Miss Sheila. There are times I let my anger and hurt rule my heart, rather than give it to the Lord. That's a dead-end road, you know."

"What do you mean?" Mom said, a note of irritation in her voice.

"Anger and bitterness only lead to pain for us and those around us. It's like weeds in a garden. It chokes out the fruit of joy and peace."

Mom looked away again. "It's hard not to give in to bitterness when you have lived a life of disappointment." She sighed. I noticed her eyes growing moist.

Marcus shook his head gently. "Oh, don't I know it, Sheila. But God is patient with us. His healing hand for our broken hearts is always there waiting for us to come to Him."

Mom remained silent, looking uncomfortable but deeply moved.

Marcus looked at Mom for a few moments, not saying anything either. I sat transfixed, nervous that Mom would suddenly get up and walk away.

Marcus spoke up. "Sheila, do you want to have peace?" He put his hand on Mom's hand.

Mom nodded, wiping away a tear. "Yes. Yes, I do."

I marveled at the situation. My stoic mother, one who rarely showed emotion other than anger or sarcasm, who never said the words "I love you" or "I'm sorry," suddenly, before my eyes, transformed into a vulnerable, genuine person. It seemed she knew this would happen and wanted it.

"Tell me about your childhood, Miss Sheila," Marcus asked.

Mom smiled, seeming to finally relax. "Well, I grew up in a large family not far from here. I had three brothers and two sisters. I was a middle child. My dad farmed and was a truck driver, and my mom took care of all of us kids and ran the garden. I remember helping Mom hang our clothes on the line with my sisters while the boys pulled weeds in the garden. On the weekends, Dad would take us down to Bull Creek to swim and fish."

"Sounds like a nice childhood," Marcus said.

Mom's smile faded. "Yes, we fought a lot but truly loved each other. Things got a lot harder after Daddy died in a car accident coming home from work. I was only twelve years old. Momma took it real hard and stayed in bed for weeks after Daddy passed."

I knew Mom's dad had died at a young age from a car accident, but this was the first time I heard Mom talk about it or her childhood. She never divulged much about her past. I never understood why.

"That must have been hard, Miss Sheila. I'm so sorry," said Marcus, shaking his head. "To lose your daddy at a tender age leaves a deep wound, I'm sure."

"Yes, it was hard. Our eldest brother, Larry, kind of took over the fatherly role with us younger siblings. He was pretty bossy!" Mom smiled.

Marcus looked at me. "Wyatt, you got a pretty special mom here. I'm sure you know that."

"Yes, I do," was all I could say, surprisingly embarrassed.

"Well, in my experience, we don't tell those we love how much we appreciate them enough. Wouldn't you agree, Miss Sheila?" Marcus asked, looking back at Mom.

Mom squirmed a little in her chair. "No, Marcus. You are right. I know in our family, the boys' father and I didn't encourage them enough. I always regretted that."

Marcus looked back at me and smiled, saying nothing.

"Tell me about your family," Mom suddenly asked Marcus. I surmised she did so to quickly change the focus off of us.

"Well, now, I've been a widow for over ten years. My wife, Betsy, was a teacher of little ones. We had two sons, both grown and living their own lives now. I got a couple of grandkids too, who must be in their teens by now."

"Do you get to see them very much?" Mom asked. "Where do they live?"

Marcus frowned and looked down momentarily, then back up at Mom. "Well, I don't get to see them too often. They live a ways away. Thomas, my elder son, lives up near Chicago, and Gabe, my younger son, lives near Memphis."

"I'm sorry. That must be hard not seeing them much."

Marcus sighed. "Yes, I do miss them, but I understand."

"So, why are you here in southern Missouri?" Mom asked.

"When we all lived in Arkansas, we liked to come up to this area for vacations. We liked to fish and camp out. Back then, we were about the only black folks in the Ozarks when we visited, but for the most part, we were treated very well. So, when it came time for me to receive longer-term care after my first stroke, I said I wanted to come here. Not sure why, to be honest."

"And eventually your boys moved to different areas I guess," I said.

"Yes. Jobs and life took them to different places. They both asked if I wanted to move to a place closer to them, but I said I was comfortable here. Sometimes I wish I had moved closer to my boys and their families, but I'm at peace. I never ever wanted to be a burden to them. They have their own kids to raise now."

I looked at Marcus' face and could see a deep sadness return. He covered it quickly with a smile, but I could see loneliness beneath the smile. I hurt for my friend.

"Well now, enough about me," Marcus said. "Miss Sheila, what do you like to do for fun these days?"

Mom grinned slightly. "Well, I like to read mysteries and watch old movies. I also like to garden but have never been too good at it."

Marcus chuckled. "Gardening was never my gift, that's for sure. I could never keep the bugs and other critters out of my crops. The only thing I could grow well was weeds!"

Mom laughed. It was good to see her enjoying her time with Marcus. I sat amazed, watching the two of them fast becoming friends.

I drove Mom home. In the car, I could tell the weight had been lifted from her shoulders. I couldn't put my finger on what that weight could be. Perhaps her loneliness weighed her down, or guilt for how she had treated us kids. I didn't know and decided not to ask her.

We pulled up to Mom's driveway. I looked at Mom.

"Did you enjoy our visit with Marcus?" I asked.

Mom smiled. "Yes, he's a very nice man. I can see why you enjoy spending time with him."

"He seemed to be taken with you too," I said. "Let me know if you want to come with me again to see him."

"I will, Wyatt," Mom said as she opened her door. She hesitated as she got out of the car, then looked back at me.

"I know I haven't been the best mom to you, Wyatt, but know I'm very proud of you."

Before I could say anything, she closed the door and walked up to her house.

As I watched her enter her house, I felt a longstanding weight lift off my heart. It seemed another dark cloud had drifted from my soul, and I saw my mother in a new light. I drove home smiling, sensing another piece of my puzzle fitting into place.

26

ETERNITY PIECE

I sat in the hospital waiting room, checking emails on my phone. The sounds of beeping and rolling wheels in the hallways, some of the wheels squeaking like an angry mother goose, added to my anxiety.

I had received a call from one of the nursing home staff that Marcus had been rushed into the emergency room after undergoing what they felt was a stroke. I had left my number with the staff since I was much closer geographically than his sons.

I thought about Marcus and all our conversations. All the pieces of his puzzle of why he believes in God and why he believes in Jesus as God's Son and our Savior. From the evidence of fine-tuning of the universe and the design of each of us to the moral code and where beauty came from—this and the other pieces had broken down many of my walls of doubt toward God. The pieces dealing with the evidence for the Bible, the life of Jesus, His death and resurrection, and the changed lives of His disciples thawed frozen places in my heart.

I realized that in the short time I had gotten to know Marcus, he had become more of a father figure in my life than my dad had ever been. Before meeting Marcus, I had never had a close black friend. Growing up and living with little to no black people, I had a skewed view of my racial bias from the opinions of relatives and friends. But after getting to know Marcus and hearing his story, I felt ashamed. Marcus was the greatest and kindest man I had ever known. Shame on me for thinking less of anyone just because of the color of their skin.

A nurse walked in and said I could see Marcus.

Fear of what I would see clasped talon-like claws into my heart. I had seen an uncle after a severe stroke, his right side completely paralyzed, and his speech slurred. My heartbeat thumped forcefully in my chest as I approached his door.

The sound of Marcus' laughter calmed my nerves as I stepped in. A nurse laughed with him as they both noticed me.

"Well, look who's here!" Marcus smiled, motioning with his right hand for me to come closer.

"Hi, Marcus," I said, fighting back tears of relief.

"Hello, Wyatt. Just having a good laugh with my friend, Nurse Rhonda!"

"How is he?" I turned to the nurse, suddenly wanting to be assured Marcus was okay.

"He's doing well. The stroke was a minor one. There doesn't seem to be any severe damage, just a little numbness on his left side that we feel will improve over time."

Air escaped out of my mouth with a deep sigh. I smiled at Marcus.

"You scared me, my friend," I said as I put my hand on his shoulder.

"Well, I must admit I scared myself!" Marcus answered, patting my hand. I'm okay, son. I'm okay."

A wave of emotion sought escape from my eyes after I heard Marcus calling me "son." I fought them back and scooted a chair next to him.

"Wyatt, I was thinking of another piece of my puzzle while

laying here that I wanted to share with you. I guess this little brush with my mortality reminded me of it. Do you have time to hear about this piece?"

I smiled. "I have all the time you need, Marcus!"

Marcus chuckled. "Good. Good then! This piece I call eternity."

"Eternity?"

"Yep. Eternity. Good timing too with me sitting in this here hospital!" Marcus chuckled again as he sat up in his bed.

"How can you prove there is a heaven and an eternity, Marcus," I asked. "It seems impossible to prove."

"True, Wyatt. I can't prove there's a heaven while we are all on this side of it, or a hell for that matter. Folks don't like talking about hell, but I believe it's just as real as heaven. Jesus talked about hell often in the Gospels."

"Okay. So how can eternity be a piece of your puzzle if you can't prove it?"

Marcus rubbed his hands together as he thought. "Well now, remember many of my pieces are not conclusive proof in and of themselves. They are just pieces. Same with eternity. I can't prove there's life beyond this one, but I believe there is evidence."

"Really?"

"Yes, sir, I do," Marcus said, nodding. "For one, there have been actual studies on near-death experiences on hundreds of patients who experienced life outside of their body."

"Wow!" I said. "That sounds pretty farfetched!"

"Several people have written about near-death experiences, or NDE," said Marcus. "Dr. Michael Sabon, who was a skeptic, did research on patients and ended up writing the books Recollections of Death and Light and Death, his account of interviews with over a hundred patients who encountered out-of-body experiences, including talking with spiritual beings and family members who have passed before."

"Well, that's one doctor," I said, still feeling skeptical.

"There's more, Wyatt," Marcus said, smiling. "Back in the early 1970s, Dr. Raymond Moody wrote the bestseller Life After Life about NDE. It seems beyond coincidence that these and other doctors, as well as individuals, have written about these experiences with amazing similarities."

"I'll have to look up those books," I said. That's interesting but not proof of a heaven, though I really hope there is."

"You are right, not conclusive proof, and I won't be able to give you that," Marcus said. "However, there is evidence. Remember the strong evidence I gave you for the reliability of the Bible?"

"Yes," I agreed.

"Well then, the Bible talks a lot about heaven as well as hell, and the reality of life after death. The resurrection is proof from Jesus that there is more to this life than our short time here. The book of Revelation reveals that eternity awaits us all."

Marcus sighed. I could tell he was getting tired.

"I should let you rest," I said, getting up.

"No, not yet. I'm enjoying talking about heaven. After all, I'm headed that way soon!" Marcus smiled.

I sat back down.

"I believe there is a deep yearning in each of us for heaven," Marcus said. "C.S. Lewis said, 'The fact that our heart yearns for something Earth can't supply is proof that heaven must be our home.' Jesus, in comforting His disciples shortly before He was arrested and crucified, promised an eternal home for them. Can you hand me my Bible over there on the table, Wyatt?"

Marcus pointed to his Bible sitting on a small table beside his hospital bed. It was worn and bent on the edges from years of use. I handed it to him. His hand, shaking slightly, grasped it, and he began turning the pages.

"Here we go. In John 14 in the first three verses, it says this:

> *Let not your hearts be troubled. Believe in God; believe also in me. In my Father's house are many rooms. If it were not so, would I have told you that I go to prepare a place for you? And if I go and prepare a place for you, I will come again and will take you to myself that where I am you may be also.*

Marcus closed his Bible. "Here Jesus promises eternal life for those who accept Him and believe in Him. In John 17:3 Jesus says eternal life is to know God and Jesus whom He sent. It's all about relationship, one that will never end, getting better and better and fuller and fuller forever and ever!"

Marcus' eyes lit up, and his voice grew louder as he finished his sentence.

"What do you think heaven will look like?" I asked, finding myself profoundly curious about this for the first time.

Marcus looked at me and took a long, deep sigh. "I think about that a lot, Wyatt, seeing that I'm going to be there soon. I do think about it a lot." He paused and looked outward, almost through me.

I waited, looking at Marcus. He seemed to have gone somewhere else, though his body remained in his bed beside me.

"I believe," Marcus suddenly continued, causing me to jump a bit, "that heaven will be a most wonderful place, one that harkens back to the best of our memories. For me, it's the quiet, reflective moments of being in nature, listening to the sounds of birds, squirrels, and insects as well as the sights of trees, deer, and flowing streams washing my pains and fears away. I believe heaven from the Bible will in the end and forever be united to earth—the new heaven and earth, fully physical and fully alive and real, more alive, and real than anything we can taste, touch, see or feel in this current world—and that our lives will be full of purpose and meaning and joy and fulfillment. It's hard to put it all into words, Wyatt, but I believe heaven will be a homecoming and a crossover into what life is supposed to be. I'm so looking forward to it!"

Marcus' words stirred something deep in my soul—a longing and a thirst that seemed natural and authentic. Thinking back over my life, I've never been totally content. Yes, there have been moments of pure joy, such as my wedding day, times with my grandma, and a few childhood memories, but none brought the total peace and happiness my soul longed for. What Marcus described just now seemed to be the water my soul's deeper thirst needed.

Marcus smiled at me. "Wyatt, I believe in my heart you will see your sister again one day. Her pain will be all gone, and you will be together forever. Be comforted in that, my friend."

Tears welled up in my eyes. The thought of seeing my sister again, happy and whole, brought a surge of hope deep inside.

"I would like that," I managed to say.

Marcus patted my hand. "And so will she, Wyatt. So will she."

I returned home but sat in my car before going inside. My conversation with Marcus galvanized new sprouts in the re-emergence of my faith. This eternity piece seemed to give fuller meaning to the picture of truth and hope in my soul. Aside from other pieces, like evidence for the resurrection of Jesus, this piece would be nothing more than a fleeting wish. But put together with the many other pieces in conversations with Marcus over the past several months, my heart was awakening to reality and truth.

I smiled as I got out of my car to tell Mary about my latest time with Marcus.

27

The Completed Puzzle

Marcus got out of the hospital, the tough old man he was. I went to visit him on a cool Saturday morning in mid-October. The leaves were just starting to change colors, and squirrels were scurrying around looking for nuts to store for the impending winter. I stared at the maple tree in front of the nursing home where Marcus and I had many conversations about God and life. The old tree reminded me of my friend—sturdy, solid, reliable, and firmly anchored. My recent years had been more like a tumbleweed, dry and blown by the winds of a broken world, with no anchor to hold me firm and secure.

Marcus had been my anchor, my root system, over this past year. He was there for me when my grandma passed. Marcus calmed me when I worried about my wife's cancer. He encouraged me in my doubts, accepted me in my anger, and showed Christ's love through all my objections. I smiled, thinking of his quick wit and laugh.

I love my friend.

Though I could tell Marcus grew weaker physically, his joy of life and rich conversation seemed only to grow fuller and more robust. I walked into his room, where he lay reading a book, his reading glasses perched low on his nose. He looked up as I walked in and smiled.

"There's the man!" he said, putting his book in his lap. "How's Wyatt doing?"

"I'm doing well, Marcus. How are you?"

"I'm living the dream! In the middle of reading *Huckleberry Finn*. That Mark Twain could write!"

I pulled up a chair close to Marcus. I noticed the eyes behind his reading glasses looked tired.

"So how is Miss Mary doing?" Marcus asked.

"She's doing great," I said. "Her pregnancy is going very well."

Marcus removed his reading glasses. "Fantastic! So glad to hear that!"

I smiled. "We are very excited. Know you were the first one we told, Marcus!"

Marcus jumped in his bed. "What? You're kidding!"

"Nope. You are now family to us, Marcus!"

Marcus smiled and quickly reached out for my hand and shook it. "Thanks, my boy! That means a lot. You and Mary are like family to me as well. I believe you and Mary are going to be fantastic parents!"

"I know Mary will be an amazing mom. I just hope I'm a better dad than mine was." My smile faded.

"Oh, Wyatt, you will be an amazing father. I can see your heart. You are full of love."

"I hope so."

"Have you told your mother?" Marcus asked.

"Yes, we told her two weeks ago. She seemed very happy about it. I have got to tell you, Marcus, since my mom met and talked with you, she has been different. She has even started going back to church again from time to time, and I've been by to see her and she's reading her Bible!"

"That's fantastic, Wyatt! I enjoyed meeting your mom. Tell her I said hello."

I looked at Marcus and his genuine smile. I admired the gentle man who, despite his declining health and lack of family involvement, still emitted such joy and compassion toward others. As I thought about all our conversations on the evidence for God and Jesus Christ being the Savior, the light in my friend's eyes and life shown to me is the most unmistakable evidence of all. I recalled the verse in 2 Corinthians 3:3, which says, "And you show that you are a letter from Christ delivered by us, written not with ink but with the Spirit of the living God, not on tablets of stone but on tablets of human hearts."

Marcus epitomized the living letter from God to me.

"So how are you really doing, Marcus?" I asked. "You've been through a lot lately."

Marcus looked at me and grinned. "Well, Wyatt, I'm not as spry as I'd like to be, that's for sure. I know my time in this old world is running short. I'm fine with that."

"Well, I'm not!" I said. "We need to finish our puzzle!"

"In fact, Wyatt, we have," Marcus said while reaching beside his bed and pulling up a drawing in a frame.

"Come closer, Wyatt. I want to show this to you."

I slid my chair closer to Marcus' bed. I noticed the pencil drawings were made to look like puzzle pieces. Inside each section were words written with Marcus' shaky handwriting.

"Now, I know you may have trouble reading my chicken scratch, so let me go over each of these pieces," Marcus said. "We've been spending time together now for a little over a year I figure, right?"

I nodded. "Yeah, that's about right."

"Ok. In that time these are the pieces of the puzzle I remember us talking about. Please remind me if I missed any."

Marcus pointed to a corner section piece. "This piece is design. Remember us talking about the fantastic design of the universe, and the unique design in each of us? The DNA in each of our cells is the blueprint for who we are, just as a blueprint for a house is obviously written out by an architect?"

"Yes, I remember," I said.

"Design points to a designer. Our design and the universe's design point to a great Designer, God."

I nodded.

Marcus pointed to another corner. "This peace is beauty. Beauty relates closely with design. A random universe could not logically produce consistent beauty as we see in creation, from the maple tree here where I live to your lovely Mary. Beauty calls for an artist, not random chance."

I thought of my wife's face and smile, gentle walk, and gorgeous legs. I had to agree. She was no accident!

Marcus pointed at another corner piece. "Here we have the fine-tuning piece for life. Remember this?"

"Yes, I remember this piece was very convincing."

"It has been for me as well, Wyatt. The odds of all the elements of fine-tuning in the universe to produce a planet that could produce life by chance is so small it really takes much more faith to believe in that than a Creator. The fine-tuning starts within the Big Bang itself and radiates out to the tilt of our planet, the distance of our moon to the earth, the material in our earth's crust, the distance of the earth from the sun . . . the list goes on and on."

I could tell Marcus was enjoying this review of his puzzle pieces. His eyes lit up despite his fatigue and shaky voice. His hands, while shaking as he pointed to the pieces, were urgent and determined.

Marcus pointed next to the final corner piece. "Here, Wyatt, we have the moral code. This was one of C.S. Lewis' favorite pieces of his puzzle. Within all of us there is this sense of right and wrong, across all cultures and times. Granted, there have been those who seemed to break this moral code, such as Hitler and Stalin. However, ingrained in all of us is this sense of fairness and truth, justice, and integrity. If we are all but random collections of molecules brought about by evolutionary processes, where does this sense of fairness come from? I believe this moral code came from a God of impeccable moral principal, the God of love and truth."

Thinking back over my life, even at the darkest moments, I never lost my sense of right and wrong. Even when questioning God, I realized it wasn't that I didn't believe in Him anymore.

I was just mad at Him.

Marcus pointed at another piece. "Here is story. Story again relates to design. As an author writes a story with a plot with characters, each of our lives seem to be woven together in family and community in a story written by someone outside of ourselves. If we are but random combinations of cells with no author, why is there story?"

I immediately thought of my favorite stories in books and films. From the book, *Eight Men in a Boat* to my all-time favorite movie, *Raiders of the Lost Ark*, these stories captured my imagination and interest from the adventure, the relationships, and overcoming adversity. Looking at my own story, I realized I had lost the sense of wonder and appreciation of how my story had adventure, relationships, and hardship to overcome.

Marcus smiled at me, realizing I was processing this review

of puzzle pieces. "Here, Wyatt, we have the piece of the puzzle called The Bible. It is important to understand how the Bible came to be, how it relates to history, how it has far more manuscripts than any other work of antiquity, how archeology has added significant reliability to the historicity of the Bible, how prophecy has shown the supernatural authority of the Bible, and how God has changed countless lives over the centuries through His written Word."

"It has helped me to realize also that the Bible is not just a single book but a collection of different types of writings," I added.

"Yes, indeed!" Marcus said. "So true. From history, prophecy, poetry, and letters, the Bible shows the overarching story of God and you and I, and His pursuit of us despite our wayward tendencies."

Marcus took a deep breath. His eyes closed.

"Are you ok?" I asked.

"Yes, I'm fine, just needing to rest a bit. When I get excited and talk a lot, I sometimes have to catch my breath."

"I can go and let you rest."

"No, I want to finish. This is important for me to finish, Wyatt."

"Ok, Marcus, but take your time."

Marcus smiled and took another deep breath. "I'm feeling better now. We've been talking about the Bible as a key piece of the puzzle why I believe in God. The central pieces deal with Jesus, who is the central focus of the Bible, from Genesis to Revelation."

"How is Jesus mentioned in Genesis?" I asked.

"In Genesis 3:15 it says, 'I will put enmity between you and the woman, and between your offspring and her offspring.

He shall bruise your head, and you shall bruise his heel.' The seed talked about here is Jesus when He defeats Satan on the cross and the resurrection."

"Wow, I didn't realize that was talking specifically about Jesus," I said.

"Yes, it does," Marcus answered. "The promise of a Messiah is mentioned throughout the Old Testament. Jesus fulfilled those predictions as the Messiah, just not in the way they expected."

"What do you mean?"

"Even Jesus' own disciples thought the Messiah would be a conquering King. They failed to realize the prophecy of Isaiah 53, which predicted the Messiah as the suffering servant who came first to die for the sins of the people, including you and I."

Marcus pointed to another section of his drawing.

"The incarnation of Jesus. The gospels of Matthew, Mark, Luke, and John share the life, death, and resurrection of Jesus as He walked on our earth over 2,000 years ago. For myself, the gospels are the heart of the message of the Bible, the core and climax of God showing His great love for us, His creation."

I smiled. "Yes, I remember this conversation. I never knew there were historians from way back who were not followers of Jesus who confirmed that He, in fact, was a real person."

"Indeed," Marcus nodded. "And the world changed dramatically as a result."

Marcus pointed to another piece in the center of the drawn-out puzzle. "The resurrection. This event in history is the single greatest event in human history, along with the incarnation and crucifixion. In the resurrection we see Jesus conquering death, thus giving each of us eternal hope that, in Christ, we will also conquer death. Eternal life is the assured hope for all who put their faith in Jesus. And the resurrection is the guaranteed seal from God that this will, indeed, be the case!"

"And the evidence for the resurrection is compelling," I chipped in.

Marcus smiled. "Oh yes. As we discussed, the evidence of the changed lives of the disciples, the empty tomb, and the multiple appearances of Jesus to many people bears strong evidence to the historical authenticity of His resurrection."

Marcus moved his hand to another section. "The changed lives of Jesus' followers are another piece of why I believe. They went from a whining group of misfits to world-changers. They went from fleeing when Jesus was arrested to brave trumpeters of Jesus' resurrection, willing to be tortured and killed rather than recant their claims."

Marcus quickly pointed to a section next to the one of the disciples' changed lives.

"As we go through history there are countless stories of lives changed by the gospel message, from Billy Graham to C.S. Lewis to Corrie Ten Boom, we find countless stories of lives utterly changed for good by the Christian message. Hearing these stories and the miracles in their own lives adds more authenticity and validity to the truth of the Gospel message."

Marcus stopped and smiled. I could tell by his eyes and voice he was growing weary.

"Do you need to rest awhile, Marcus?" I asked

"Oh no, I'm fine," Marcus said, patting my hand. "I just need to catch my breath."

I stared at my friend. His weathered hands both quivered on his lap, and his lips trembled slightly. I could see Marcus' body growing weaker, and sadness suddenly enveloped me. I wondered how much more time we would have together.

"This next piece," Marcus said, "is the ringing of the trueness of the Christian message. Remember our conversation on this?"

"Yes, I do," I said. "I remember you encouraging me to dig deep in the Gospels to see the heart of God in the life of Jesus, and from that encounter see if it did not ring true."

"And did you take my challenge?" Marcus asked.

"Well, not totally yet" I said. I have been reading in John lately, but not daily."

"That's okay, Wyatt. Keep at it," Marcus encouraged.

Marcus pointed to the next section. "This piece is one most don't like talking about. Embracing the mystery. Some things that happen in life are hard and unfair and we don't know why a loving God would accept them."

"Yes, this piece is still very hard for me," I said.

"I understand, Wyatt. The key is learning to accept the fact that we in our limited vision and perspective cannot understand all the whys in life. We also need to understand we live in a broken world that has rebelled against the Creator. We are told from Scripture that the rain will fall on the righteous as well as the unrighteous here."

"Yes, but sometimes that rain feels like acid rain," I said.

"I know, Wyatt, but remember that God Himself came to the earth in Jesus to take on all that pain and brokenness for each of us. God doesn't shield Himself from our pain; He came and took it on. He is a God of empathy, not just sympathy."

Marcus' last words struck my heart like a bolt of lightning.

God is a God of empathy, not just sympathy. Those words touched my heart deeply.

"Finally," Marcus said, "we discussed the piece on God putting eternity into our hearts. The idea of life beyond this life that will never end seems right and brings deep hope."

"Yes, it does," I said. "The idea of seeing my sister again fills me with hope."

"Yes, Wyatt. The idea of seeing my momma and wife again fills me with hope too. I can't wait for the reunion!"

Marcus looked at me and smiled. "All these pieces fit together have formed a picture in my mind of the ultimate truth that God is real, alive, and loves you and me and all of His children. All these pieces form a picture that clearly shows who God is and what He is like."

With that, Marcus picked up the picture from his lap and turned it over. It showed a close-up picture of Jesus staring at me with earnest, kind eyes, darkened tanned skin, unkempt hair, and a slight smile. My eyes watered as I realized the reality of what Marcus was saying.

"Truth is not a concept, Wyatt," Marcus said with deep emotion in his voice. "It is a person. Truth is not a set of rules but an invitation to a relationship. All these pieces put together show a God of love embodied in Jesus reaching down to you and me. This is why I believe."

I suddenly began to cry, realizing that I too now truly and fully believed. The pieces finally fit together.

28

A Sudden Goodbye

After my time with Marcus looking at the completed picture of why he believed and how the pieces of belief formed the image of Jesus, I felt compelled to share my findings with my mom. Her newfound faith had brought us closer together, healing some old wounds but not all.

I pulled into her driveway, expecting her to be sitting on her front porch smoking and smiling at me. She wasn't there. I knocked on her door. "Mom, it's Wyatt," I called. No answer.

I checked the door and saw it was unlocked, so I stepped in. The house was eerily quiet. "Mom, it's Wyatt," I said again as I stepped from the kitchen into the living room. The house remained silent and stoic. The heaviness of the air surprised me. My heart started beating faster. All the lights were off. I walked down the hallway and noticed Mom's bedroom door was open. I called her name again. Nothing. Slowly I stepped into the room, where I saw her lie.

And I knew.

Mom lay silently on her back with her eyes slightly opened. Her hands lay crossed over her chest. Her face looked rigid, like the face of a statue.

I slowly got on my knees and knelt before my mother, tears coming out of my eyes like soldiers crawling one by one out of a burrow. My breathing became labored, and sobs etched out of my throat.

My mom was gone.

Memories came cascading down, waves of both good and bad. Mom's often harsh words and cold demeanor etched deep wounds in my soul growing up. However, our relationship over the past year had gradually grown close, with Mom's recent visit with Marcus creating a definite turning point. In the end, her heart had softened toward Christ, and peace had finally entered her life, knowing she was loved and forgiven.

I held my mother's hand and stared at her face, weathered and worn from a life beset with sorrow and setbacks. Though she showed little love to me and my siblings growing up, she was my mom. A deep ache traveled deep into the recesses of my mind, from the little boy tagging behind her at the grocery store to the young man fixing her gutters. An essential piece of the person I was and will be had left.

We found out later Mom had died in her sleep of a massive stroke. She would have encountered no pain, the doctor said. As the EMTs wheeled Mom's body out of her house, I called Mary.

We had a funeral to plan.

Marcus sighed when I told him of Mom's passing.

"I'm so sorry, Wyatt. I remember my mom's passing like it was yesterday. There's a deep sadness to lose your momma."

"Thanks, Marcus. It helps knowing she knew Christ and is at deep peace now. She had a rough life."

Marcus patted my hand. "And you were a good son to her until the end. Know that."

"I hope so," I said, my voice cracking.

A smattering of folks from the area attended Mom's

funeral, along with relatives. All my siblings attended. It was good to see everyone, and after the funeral, we enjoyed sharing stories of growing up. We didn't mention Dad much but relished stories of sneaking out of the house and other adventures without our parents' knowledge.

The following day after the funeral, I rose early in the morning, unable to fall back asleep. I decided to go for a walk in the woods near our house. A few days before, a fall chill brought a killer frost with the welcoming effect of killing the ticks and chiggers.

I walked in silence, listening to the gentle crunch of my feet on the fallen leaves of the forest. Memories rushed back of treks through the woods as a youngster, exploring the wooded arena, and looking for wildlife and imagining adventure. The woods also brought solace to my bruised heart, beaten by harsh words from my mom or silent scorn from my dad, rejection from the pretty girl I had a crush on in school, or the simple insecurity of seeing myself in the mirror and wondering if anyone would ever truly know me.

I walked this morning thinking of my childhood, at times terribly lonely, even with brothers, with no strong father figure in my life. I walked this morning thinking of my life now, with a wife I deeply loved, a child on the way where I could rectify the mistakes of my own father, and a new father figure in Marcus, a gentle, kind, older man who had helped put the broken pieces of my life back together into a cohesive picture.

I stopped suddenly and noticed a doe through the many trees down below, sipping water in a small stream. She looked up and stared at me. Her big brown eyes seemed not to blink. I stood transfixed, soaking in a moment of wonder. The piece of the puzzle called beauty came to mind as I observed this amazing product of creation. I smiled, overcome suddenly with a peace that washed over me like a cleansing spring rain, removing doubts, pain, and regrets. I felt God was telling me in His still, small voice that He was there and would never leave me.

I suddenly remembered Marcus' story of the deer when he was about to take his life and the deer appearing in front of us at the end of the story. Tears welled up in my eyes, realizing God was reminding me again that He cared for me and was here with me at this tender moment.

My foot shifted a tiny bit, and the crunch of a single leaf caused the doe to suddenly bolt, turn, and run deeper into the wood. I watched and listened to the crashing leaves and limbs as the deer escaped our encounter.

I remained still, basking in the moment, listening to my breaths, and smelling the fragrance of the trees and flowers mingled together. God's love and peace wrapped around me like a warm blanket, holding me and comforting me in my grief.

After a few minutes, I continued walking in silence, grateful for my encounter and reminder of a God who listens to our hearts.

29

The Next Spring

I held my wife's hand with my right hand while holding our newborn baby boy, Steven, in my left arm. We stood at the gravesite of my dear friend, Marcus. Marcus passed away a month before gently in his sleep. The nursing home called me soon after reaching his family. I traveled to the place where Marcus was born and where we visited. I got to meet his kids. They all seemed very appreciative of me and my friendship with Marcus.

I read the words on his gravestone, "The truth shall set you free." In my heart, I knew Marcus was, indeed, free. I could picture him and my mom visiting and laughing, with the weight of each of their pain in this broken world lifted. I'm not sure if Marcus still battled with puzzles in heaven, but if so, he had all the time in eternity to work on it. I smiled thinking about that.

Mary looked at me. "Are you okay, honey?"

I squeezed her hand. "I'm okay. Thanks for going with me on this long drive to see my friend."

"Of course. God used this kind man to change both our lives. To me, Marcus is family."

I nodded. "Indeed, he's the dad I never really had."

My voice cracked.

We drove home in silence while Steven slept peacefully in

the back. I remembered my trip with Marcus on this road to visit his hometown. I could still hear his laughter as he recalled happy childhood memories with his brothers. Our racial barrier had melted away over the love and acceptance he showed me from the start.

The color of our skin became not a wall but a bridge—a bridge of understanding each other's culture and background, a bridge of embracing our diversity by the unifying love of Christ. It took me a while to get there. Still, through Marcus' consistent, caring concern about Mary and me, I grew to embrace the man Marcus was—a man of faith and compassion. My friend.

My friend showed me the pieces of his life, the pieces of why he believed in God, and how those pieces helped put the pieces of his heart back together. His words and our relationship helped me do the same.

I thought about my son, and how I was committed to breaking the cycle I grew up with. My son would hear the words "I love you" often. I would teach him about God and His exceptional character, of Jesus and the life He lived, the death He gave, and the resurrection that pointed the way to ultimate hope and purpose in this broken world. I heard Steven cooing in the back and smiled. I welcomed the challenge and adventure of being his dad.

As we drove, I observed the late spring afternoon. Trees were budding everywhere, and new grass shone brightly, offering new life and hope. Birds danced from tree to tree, and butterflies floated by my windshield. I rolled my window down to breathe in the fragrance of flowers and pine mingled with the warm afternoon breeze.

We approached a Dollar General, and I suddenly pulled into the parking lot.

"What are you doing?" Mary asked.

"I'll be just a minute," I said as I unbuckled my seat belt.

I returned a few minutes later with my bag.

"What did you get?" Mary asked.

I slowly pulled my purchase out of the bag and smiled as I showed it to Mary.

It was a puzzle.

List of Works Researched for This Book

Brand, Paul and Yancey, Philip. *Fearfully and Wonderfully*. Downers Grove: InterVarsity Press, 2019.

Habermas, Gary and Licona, Michael. *The Case for the Resurrection of Jesus*. Grand Rapids: Kregel Publications, 2004.

Lindsley, Art. *C.S. Lewis's Case for Christ*. Downer's Grove: InterVarsity Press, 2005.

Little, Paul. *Know Why You Believe*. Downers Grove: InterVarsity Press, 1968.

McDowell, Josh. *More Than a Carpenter*. Wheaton: Tyndall House Publishing, Inc., 1977.

McDowell, Josh and McDowell, Sean. *Evidence That Demands a Verdict*. Nashville: Thomas Nelson, 2017.

Moreland, J.P. *Love Your God With All Your Mind*. Colorado Springs: NavPress, 1997.

Morrison, Frank. *Who Moved the Stone?* Grand Rapids: Zondervan, 1958.

Ross, Hugh. *The Creator and the Cosmos*. Colorado Springs: NavPress, 1993.

Strobel, Lee. *The Case for Christ*. Grand Rapids: Zondervan, 1998.

Strobel, Lee. *The Case for Faith*. Grand Rapids: Zondervan, 2000.

Strobel, Lee. *The Case for a Creator*. Grand Rapids: Zondervan, 2004.

Wallace, J. Warner. *Cold-Case Christianity*. Colorado Springs: David C Cook, 2013.

Wright, N.T. *The Resurrection of the Son of God*. Minneapolis: Fortress Press, 2003.

About the Author

GREG STONE, with his beloved wife, Jodi, of over 31 years, live near Branson, Missouri on the land where he grew up. They have two grown sons, Casey with wife, Abigail, and Drew with wife, Faith, and one grandson, Jack.

Greg is presently the associate regional director for Young Life, helping to oversee the Gateway Region of Missouri. In his spare time, Greg enjoys reading, writing, watching St. Louis Cardinals baseball and Kansas City Chiefs football, and spending time with his wife and family.

To contact Greg email him at gstone0429@gmail.com, or message his author facebook page at https://www.facebook.com/G.A.Stone0429.